THE NOBLE ADVENTURES

OF

BERYL AND CAROL

park

town

school

Old Dust Road

Carol's house

Beryl's house

Mrs E

To my four Gorgeous Girlies, who inspired this story out of me and carried me all the way through: Ella Naomi, Tilly Jane, Noga Lily, and Amy Grace

THE NOBLE ADVENTURES

OF

Beryl & Carol

JEREMY SHERR

Book Cover by Talya Baldwin

Illustrations by Talya Baldwin

"*Every act of strength leads to another act of strength*
Every act of weakness leads to another act of weakness
Courage begets courage
Fear breeds fear."
— *Carol's Dad*

CHAPTER 1

Beryl was not sure they had escaped, so she glanced behind, listening for any sounds. Nothing yet. They had reached the end of the Old Dust Road. Beryl had managed to keep the rusty tin can rolling for the last two miles, but now they were at a dead end. She dished out a final nasty kick, and the can cluttered noisily into the gutter. She dragged herself to the edge of the path, feeling like a prisoner on death row.

Carol followed, looking as miserable as the tin can.

A moment later, the girls heard the awful sound of Earnie's croaky laugh from not far behind. They *were* being followed, and it would not be long before the bullies caught up with them. They looked around, frantically searching for a way out. There was none. On their left were open fields, up ahead the forest, and behind them the road, down which their tormentors were fast approaching. There was no way back, nowhere to hide, and certainly no going into the forest. The girls stood paralysed, their legs trembling like fresh jelly. Beryl could taste the fear in her mouth, and Carol's heart was pounding like a jackhammer. They were caught between being tortured for hours and a dark Forbidden Forest, which was not an option.

Carol scowled at Beryl. She looked upset, angry, and scared, and she was trying to shout and whisper at the same time.

"Look what you've gotten us into, dork! You and your big ideas. If they catch us here, we're totally trapped. We'll spend the rest of the afternoon having our hair pulled, dirt and stones stuck down our collars, our bags emptied, and all our stuff kicked around in the dust. Only this time, there'll be no one around to help."

Beryl looked at the ground, feeling as though her aunt had just told her off. It was true that she had suggested escaping from the school's back gate, even though they both knew it was a dead end. But it had only been a week since the boys had snatched Carol's bag and scattered her stuff all over the schoolyard, kicking her private things around like a football. Beryl just couldn't stand being humiliated in front of the whole school again, and escaping through the back gate had seemed like a good idea at the time. The back gate had led to the dust road, the dust road had coughed up the tin can, and the tin can had lured them to the edge of the Forbidden Forest. They knew it would not take long for the boys to work out how they had escaped, and most likely, they would follow them, as they had nothing better to do. Now, Beryl and Carol were stuck and about to get a beating.

The boys' voices were growing louder. They would arrive at any moment.

Suddenly, Beryl grabbed Carol by the sleeve and whispered, "Into the forest. Now!"

"What? You're mad!" Carol pulled her arm away, alarmed by yet another of Beryl's stupid ideas. "You know no one's allowed in the forest." Carol was almost 12, three months older than Beryl, so she considered herself to be the 'responsible adult,' which is precisely what made Beryl more rebellious.

"Why not?!" Beryl glared at her urgently. "Who's going to know? Unless you tell someone, of course."

"You know I would never do that." Carol blushed. "It's just…"

"Just, just, just," Beryl imitated her. "Come on, let's go."

Carol rolled her eyes, ready to argue against Beryl's second crazy move of the day. But just then, they heard the boys' laughing and jeering coming from behind the last bend in the road. They had thirty seconds at most.

Beryl had done enough talking. She pulled a rude face, then turned and bolted into the forest, leaving a stunned and reluctant Carol with no choice but to run after her. Carol would rather have faced an afternoon with the bullies than go into the forest, but there was no way she was letting Beryl go in there alone.

This was the first time either of the girls had been beyond the tree line. In fact, it was the first time *anyone* had been beyond the tree line for many, many years. It felt like jumping off the edge of the universe.

At that moment, the two friends never imagined they were walking into the biggest adventure of their lives.

CHAPTER 2

The two girls crouched low behind a thick bush just inside the forest, waiting anxiously and careful not to make the slightest sound. Beyond the last line of trees, they could see the boys arriving at the end of the dust road, nasty grins plastered all over their faces. When they did not find their victims where they had expected them to be, they looked around with dumbfounded expressions, scratching their heads. One of them uttered an unrepeatable word. They were obviously surprised and upset that their afternoon entertainment had escaped.

"Must've snuck round the school." Gimpy looked puzzled.

That didn't make sense, so the boys suggested a few increasingly far-fetched theories, which finally deteriorated into Earnie's 'dug a hole in the ground' idea and Simon's 'kidnapped by flying saucers.' For a moment, the girls smirked inwardly, realising they had outsmarted their tormentors.

"Never mind, we'll get them tomorrow," declared Simon, aimlessly throwing a stone into the woods. The stone whizzed dangerously close to Beryl's head, forcing the girls to squat even lower, terrified.

Beryl and Carol huddled together as they listened to the bullies devising various plans to 'get' them. These involved more grass ambushes, with the delightful addition of mud mixed with thorns and cow dung. Carol shivered, and Beryl's pale face went red, but they dared not move.

Beryl and Carol were not quite sure why the bullies always picked on them.

"Maybe they're in love with us," Carol had suggested one day, and Beryl had made the face of someone who had just eaten a lemon. But they both knew the sad truth. The three boys, who liked to call themselves the 'High-Street Gang,' were two years older and much stronger, so the girls were easy victims. They had been harassing them for the last three years, and Beryl and Carol had been too scared to fight back or tell their parents, so it just got worse every day.

The two friends crouched low, holding hands and waiting for the boys to get tired and go home so they could escape the forest as quickly as possible.

But that didn't seem to be happening.

"Let's light a fire," they heard Earnie suggest. The girls could smell cigarette smoke.

"Cool," echoed Gimpy and Simon, who usually followed Earnie's lead.

The boys walked to the other side of the road to find dry wood. Naturally, they were not going to search for wood in the Forbidden Forest.

Beryl realised this was their one and only chance to escape. She tugged Carol by the sleeve and made a Let's-get-out-of-here gesture with her head.

Carol was about to protest, but this time she knew that her friend was right. It was now or never. If they didn't move immediately, they would be stuck in the same spot till after dark. That would mean big trouble at home. Beryl signalled to Carol with her hand that they would try to circle round and exit the forest at a different point. Carol nodded reluctantly. It was their only hope.

Just before the boys returned with the firewood, the two friends turned and, crawling on their hands and knees, edged deeper into the dark forest. The earth was rough. Stones and thorns tore their jeans and scratched their knees and elbows. They had never been so scared in their lives.

CHAPTER 3

Beryl and Carol continued crawling until the boys' voices faded away. But the bullies were no longer their biggest problem. They were deep in the Forbidden Forest, which felt as though all their worst nightmares had merged into one and swallowed them up. The spooky pine trees looked at them sternly as if to say, 'What are you two doing here?!' The shrill, cold March wind whistled through leaves and branches, sending icicles up their spines and goosebumps onto their skin. The girls huddled closer together. This was the last place in the world they wanted to be. Everyone in town knew the forest was a no-go area. Everybody knew why, but nobody dared speak about it anymore.

The two girls looked at each other with terror. There was no doubt they had made a serious blunder. Maybe a fatal one. As bad as facing the boys had seemed, it would have been far better than entering the dreaded forest. At least they would be dealing with familiar enemies rather than deadly robbers and murderers.

They tiptoed through the trees, stepping cautiously, so they did not break a branch or crush a leaf underfoot. Every few moments, they stopped and peered around. The forest was overgrown and unkept. Between the trees were thick clumps of bushes and protruding roots that made walking increasingly difficult. Jagged pine branches reached out, scratching their arms and legs. They could hear the groaning of tree trunks, creaking branches, rustling leaves, and birds flapping above. Each of these noises was amplified a thousand times in the girls' minds.

Suddenly, they heard a twig snap and something scuttle along the ground. Carol grasped Beryl's arm so tightly that Beryl nearly screamed, but she managed to keep quiet. They stood still, listening. Every crackle became a smuggler; every snap became a murderer, every crunch was a werewolf. As they penetrated deeper into the woods, the trees rose tall and thick around them, so it seemed almost dark, even though it was still early afternoon. The darkness only increased their fear. They had got themselves into an awful situation. Carol imagined a root suddenly curling around her leg and pulling her into the ground.

Beryl pointed to the right, hoping they might find a way out of the forest further along, though this was just a guess. Carol followed. After a few moments of creeping along, the girls came across a small path, so they turned and followed that. Carol wondered who had cleared the trail, but that did not matter now. All that mattered was getting out there. The going on the path was slightly more comfort- able, and there was enough distance between them and the boys to walk a bit faster.

When they felt they had gone far enough, the girls stopped to talk for the first time since entering the forest.

"Stupid, stupid, stupid!" Carol glared at Beryl. It was all HER fault. Only five minutes ago, they had been walking down the old dust road kicking a tin can. And now they were at the gates of hell.

Beryl had nothing to say. It had been a crazy move.

"I'm really scared." Carol's voice was trembling. "You know what happened to Tim."

"Of course I know. Everybody knows. But, Carol, it's 1997 now. What happened to Tim is ancient history, way back in 1982." She thought for a second. "That's fifteen years ago!" Beryl tried to sound confident, but Carol knew her friend was just as frightened as she was.

Escaping the High-Street Gang into the forest was like jumping from a frying pan into a volcano, except they were so frozen with fear even a volcano would not have thawed them.

"Do you think we can find our way back out?" Beryl whispered, trying to sound brave, but there was a clear tremble in her voice.

This was exactly what Carol had been wondering. She did not have an answer.

"How about we leave a trail?" Carol looked around. "Maybe breadcrumbs from our sandwiches?" As soon as she said it, they both knew this was a bad idea.

"Nonco," said Beryl. "You know the story…"

'Nonco' was the fun name the girls teased each other with. It more or less meant, 'You are an idiot, but I love you anyway.' No one was sure where it came from initially, but it always made them smile. Beryl's mum claimed it began when Carol was a toddler; she would say 'no-go,' 'no-go,' when she was visiting Beryl and had to go home. The girls had practically lived together since they could crawl. Even though Beryl was younger, she was taller than Carol. As she often reminded her best friend, three months younger was not going to make her shorter. Half-Finnish Beryl was tall and thin with long blonde hair and blue eyes. Carol had a darker complexion, wavy brown hair and deep green eyes, so it was easy to tell them apart. Although they were hardly ever apart.

"Yes, yes," Carol interrupted, waving her hand awkwardly. "I know the story of 'Hansel and Gretel.' I was just checking if you knew…"

Beryl pulled a face. She knew when her friend was lying, kidding, or pulling her leg.

"I have a better idea." Beryl looked for something sharp on the ground. "Let's make marks on the trees."

That made sense. Beryl picked up a stone with a sharp edge,

and Carol pulled out a coin, and they used these to scratch marks on the trees as they walked down the path, still hoping it would lead them out of the woods. The sinister pines had thankfully given way to more native English trees—birch, elms, ash, and others whose names they did not know. It was a beautiful forest, and though their hearts were still racing, somehow, they could not turn back. It was as if the forest had caught them in its web and was pulling them inwards. They walked on in silence, stopping now and then to mark a tree and look around.

Beryl glanced at her watch. 4:15 PM. It had been about half an hour since they had entered the forest. It was mid-March, and the days were just beginning to lengthen, but they knew it would be dark soon, and their fear grew. Only an hour and a half of daylight left to get out. They were thinking about Tim and were terrified of being lost in the woods after dark. But the unknown dangers surrounding them were not the only reason the girls were anxious. If their parents ever even found out they had entered the forest, it would spell big trouble. The forest was big, dark, and unknown, so they could easily get lost inside. This would result in general panic and police and search parties, helicopters and TV crews, followed by horrible punishments—probably curfew for a year, with washing up.

"Do you think we should turn…?" Beryl seemed scared.

Carol, grateful that it was Beryl who had chickened out first, was just about to pretend to reluctantly agree to go back when they both heard it. From their left came a low rumbling sound, too faint to identify. They stood still, trying to work out what it was, not daring to move but getting ready to run. Perhaps it was an animal snarling or even a person! The growling continued, sometimes louder and sometimes softer. Carol squeezed Beryl's hand until it hurt, and Beryl looked around for somewhere to hide or a tree to climb.

CHAPTER 4

T he noise came and went, sometimes there, other times masked by the wind rustling through the leaves. The two girls listened intently but could not work out what it was or where it was coming from. Suddenly, the wind died down, and they could hear the sound clearly.

"Wait…" Carol put a finger to her lips and cocked her head to one side. Then her eyes lit up, and a grateful smile spread over her face. "Beryl, it's our river!" she beamed.

Both girls were immediately relieved, as if they had just met an old friend who was going to take them home. The river, their river! The river flowed past their backyards and was their best friend. Ever since they could remember, they had played on its banks, thrown mud balls into the water, tried to catch fish with sticks and string, sailed paper boats and leaves with twig masts under the small bridge. In the summer, they would jump in and swim about, laughing and splashing in the cool water. It was the bubbling song of the river that sang them a lullaby every night, wrapping them with sleepiness before their heads touched the pillow. They loved the river! If the river was close, they could find their way home.

Carol scratched a mark on a nearby tree, and the two girls followed the sound into the woods. The branches were low and thick, and they struggled to get through, often stumbling on roots and getting pricked by thorny bushes. Beryl wished they had a big machete to hack at the growth.

It took them seven or eight minutes to get close to the river. They could hear its rushing waters nearby, and when they climbed over a final large root, they were finally by its side. "Oh, river," Carol let out a sigh of relief. The girls immediately felt safer.

The river seemed narrower here than where it met their houses, but it was their river, for sure. They had never known where it came from because they were not allowed to follow it into the woods. Now they knew. It felt so comfortable, a world apart from the terror that had grasped them moments ago. The girls sat on the riverbank for a few minutes, watching its tumbling waters toss and turn, swirling around fallen branches and rocks, white eddies decorating the rims like icing on a cake. In any other situation, they would have sat gazing at the water for hours, but they were anxious to get home before dark, or they would be lost in the woods, and their parents would be beside themselves with worry and anger. The girls knew it was at least 45 minutes to the edge of the forest if they returned the way they had come. It would be dark, and they would not be able to see the marks on the trees. And the bullies might still be there.

They were silent for a moment, and then Carol said, "Only one way we can…"

"Yes." Beryl pointed down the riverbank. "Down the river."

"Do you think it will get us home?" Carol was unsure.

"Of course, Nonco." Beryl stood up. "This is our river. It has to take us home."

"Let's follow it downstream." Carol got up from her riverbank seat and wiped the mud off her pants.

"Too slow, Nonco. I'm on my way." Beryl had begun scrambling along the bank.

"You shut up!" Carol followed. It was another of their favourite sayings, and they both smiled.

Progress was not easy. There was no path, just the slippery

riverbank, and the two girls had to hold on to branches to avoid falling in. Nettles, bushes and roots were growing all along the bank, and big trees and rocks blocked their way. The hopes gained from finding the river were now dashed on its banks. Moving forward was slow, and it would take them hours to get home. They would be trapped in the dark forest all night, maybe longer. Carol imagined her parents going frantic at home. All Beryl could think of was being found by a search party and facing horrible TV crews outside her house.

They followed the riverbank but reached a rocky area that they could not pass, forcing them to clamber away from the bank and climb over an old fallen tree.

Then they saw it, and their jaws dropped wide open.

CHAPTER 5

Before them was a large clearing in the forest. It was a garden of colour; green grass carpeted with whites, pinks, and yellows and framed with hues of blue. Beryl, who knew the names of flowers, recognised golden celandine, white snowdrops, and primroses. Around the edges, early bluebells flowered. The clearing was surrounded by trees, rowan and hawthorn and poplar, some decorated with white mistletoe berries. To one side, their beloved river bubbled, and over it, a large willow hung its long, delicate branches. But, best of all was the giant tree. It was a red oak, and it was humongous. It stood close by the riverbank, its trunk the size of Carol's bedroom, its massive branches spanning over to the opposite bank, its canopy forming a dome over the grass below. The whole clearing was shining in the gentle evening sunlight, lighting the wild grass and flowers with a magical glow. It was so beautiful it took their breath away.

The girls just stood and stared, spellbound. They had never seen anything so beautiful in their lives. It felt as though they had suddenly been transported to another world.

After a few minutes that seemed like hours, they moved into the middle of the clearing, walking softly so as not to break the spell or crush any flowers. It was even more gorgeous from here, a sparkling carpet of spring flowers garnished with the sweet smell of wild garlic. Not saying a word, the girls explored the clearing, staring at the grass and flowers and trees, smelling the sweet scents, gazing at the great oak which crowned it all.

Carol was first to speak, but all she managed to utter was: "No way!"

"No way," Beryl echoed softly.

The two girls looked at each other, almost crying from happiness. Slowly, big grins spread across their faces, and they began to laugh. Carol lay down on the grass and stretched out her arms and legs, and Beryl was quick to do the same, lying on her back and gazing at the clouds floating beyond the oak's branches.

It was a magic garden! Better still, it was a *secret* magic garden.

They could have stayed in their newfound paradise forever, but the sun was beginning to melt into the trees, and the girls remembered their situation. Beryl stood up, wiped the grass off her clothes, and reluctantly murmured, "We better get home."

They took one last look at the beautiful clearing, then returned to the riverbank and started to make their way downstream. The going was difficult. The bank was slippery and covered in roots and nettles, though it was too early in the year for them to sting. Twice they had to wade knee-deep into the water so they could cross a fallen tree or rock. The mountain snows had been melting, so the water was freezing and flowing fast.

Evening began to turn into night, and they pushed on faster. Twenty minutes had passed since they had left the clearing, and they were starting to doubt whether the river would get them home. The girls were scared. It became difficult to see the bushes and roots in the dark, and once or twice, they stumbled and fell. Their hands were scratched, their shoes, socks, and jeans were soaked, and they were cold and tired. At one point, Beryl slipped on the smooth stones underfoot and into the water, grabbing hold of Carol and nearly dragging her in, but they managed to catch a low branch and pull themselves back onto the bank, panting and shivering from cold.

They were desperate. Soon their parents would begin to worry and then call the police…

All the girls wanted to do was give up, but they had to push on—just one more bend in the riverbank, and another, and one more. And finally, there they were, the flickering lights of the last house in the village, and close behind, Beryl and Carol's twin cottages, nestled back to back.

They were home! The girls felt an enormous relief—this was their river, it did bring them home, and they were safe! That is, safe from the woods. But not yet safe from their parents.

Since they were little, their parents, fearful of a drowning accident, had warned the two friends to stay away from the river at night. Beryl and Carol had broken every rule in the book. They had to get into their homes without being seen. Not easy!

"M-m-m- my parents will be watching TV." The frozen Beryl barely managed to squeeze the words past her chattering teeth. "L-l-l-let's sneak in the back door and get changed. If they see us wet from the river, we are toast!"

Actually, toast sounded like heaven to the trembling Carol.

They sneaked past the last house, sitting right on the riverbank. Through the window, they could see Mrs. Ecclestone busy in her kitchen, and they both longed for her hug and warm smile, carrot cake and hot chocolate. But now was not the time, and they moved stealthily onto Beryl's back gate and up the garden path, bending low so as not to be seen. Beryl had her opening-the-back-door-quietly technique down to a fine art, and soon they were creeping up the stairs and into her room. Fortunately, Sam was not there. They had no time for a shower, so they just dried quickly and changed clothes. Carol borrowed a sweatshirt (which was probably hers anyway, as they shared everything) and some jeans which were too long, so she rolled up the legs to fit her.

When the girls were dry and changed, they came down the

stairs noisily.

"Where have you two been?" Beryl's mum called from the TV couch.

"Oh, just playing 'magic garden' in my room," Beryl called back. The girls looked at each other, trying hard not to laugh. Silently, they did the short version of their secret handshake, and Carol rushed home.

They were both exhausted, but neither girl would sleep much that night.

CHAPTER 6

The next morning when they met on the way to school, the two friends were bubbling with ideas and excitement.

"Wow!" said Carol.

"Wow!" Beryl hi-fived.

A few more 'wows' followed.

"I've been thinking about it all night," Carol said excitedly.

"Me too!" gushed Beryl.

"That place is stonking." Stonking was another word they both loved.

"Absolutely amazing," replied Beryl. "And best of all, no one knows about it, and let's hope no one ever will!"

They looked at each other and grinned. There was so much to say.

"Let's go back as soon as we can," said Beryl.

"For sure," replied Carol. "And listen to this. I checked on the map. We can get to the same forest path through the back corner of the park. It's a bit longer, but we don't have to go down the old dust road."

"Excellent." Beryl was pleased. "We can't go today, 'cause I have basketball, and you have swimming, and the day after tomorrow is the stupid maths exam. But how about a picnic on the weekend?"

Carol loved her swimming, and Beryl never missed a basketball practice. She was passionate about the game and was mid-school captain. But the weekend sounded good.

"Picnic it is!" Beryl settled it. "And I have some other ideas."

Suddenly, they were being covered with grass cuttings from all sides.

"Take that!" and "Here's some more!" and "Eat this!"

Usually, the two friends were aware of exactly where the boys would be waiting in ambush, but they had been so busy chatting about their garden that they had forgotten to be careful. The Gang had been hiding behind a wall, and they jumped out and threw wads of freshly cut grass at the girls. The fat one, Ernie, even managed to get some down Beryl's collar. The girls screamed and ran. They were covered in grass again, and Beryl's neck would be itching all day.

"Beryl and Peril, Beryl and Peril," the boys chanted after them as they ran.

Carol winced. The boys had started calling her Peril a few weeks ago, based on the *Beryl the Peril* comic. In fact, she was first nicknamed the 'Peril' by Beryl's parents when she was little after she had spent all morning preparing 30 mud balls and then thrown them at Beryl's newly painted house. The nickname had stuck, and it had now been catching on at school. Carol secretly liked being called Peril because she loved the comic character, but also because she was considered a 'goody' at school. She thought that being named Peril showed her other side, which she liked to think of as daring with a touch of naughty. Still, that didn't give the bullies the right to call her that.

It was not until after school that the girls could talk again.

"I'm going to kill those boys," Beryl spluttered, scratching her neck. "I can't understand why they hate us so much."

"Maybe because Earnie's brother bullies him, and they're all rubbish at sports, and no one in their class likes them, and they haven't got a life. Bullies have often been bullied themselves." Carol slipped into psychologist mode.

"Maybe, whatever, but we aren't bullies, and to be honest, I don't care why they are. We just have to stop this," Beryl moaned. "Why not ask Jerry to deal with them?" Jerry was Carol's older brother.

"No chance. Jerry bullies me as well. He would just laugh," said Carol with a scowl, pulling another bit of grass out of her collar. You could never get rid of it all until you showered and changed clothes. "But we beat them once, so we can beat them again. I have a better plan."

So, off they went to the park to discuss Carol's plan and the weekend picnic. They sat in their 'office,' a bench at the end of the park, hidden behind some trees. Carol began a list of what to bring to the picnic.

"Not too much," she said while writing, "It's a long way, so we can't take anything heavy."

"Well, here comes my great idea," Beryl said enthusiastically. "How about we leave some stuff there?"

"Brilliant!" replied Carol, miffed that she had not thought about that herself.

"Tell you what." Beryl was bubbling. "Every time we go for a picnic, we take some extra stuff. We can hide it there, and then we won't have to carry things the next time."

They got out a pencil and paper, and Carol, who could never resist a list, made a line down the middle and then two columns on either side.

It looked like this:

Stuff to bring once	Who	Stuff to leave there	Who
Sandwiches	B&C	Blanket	C
Juice	B	Cups	B
Thermos with tea (milk, no sugar)	C	2 Forks 2 spoons 2 knives	B
Fruit	C	Cards	C
Salad	C	Ball	C
Paper napkins	C	Backgammon	B
Cake	Beryl's mum	Frisbee	B
TWITW	C	Towels	C

The girls tried to spread the list evenly between the two of them. Still, there was no doubt that it would have to be Beryl's mum's cake, simply because she made the best one (chocolate with orange juice as opposed to Carol's mum's dry sponge cake). They were going to add more things to the list but realised that would be all they could carry.

"Never mind," said Carol, "there'll be plenty more times. But right now, we have to get ready for tomorrow's big plan!"

CHAPTER 7

Beryl and Carol were silent and tense. They had to time events carefully for their plan to work. Both were holding the big mud cakes they had prepared, and as they got nearer to the bullies' wall, they got ready to throw them. They knew exactly where they would be hiding; boys were sooo predictable.

Quietly, they crept to the edge of the wall and then, on a signal from Carol, began to lob the mud cakes over the fence to where they were sure the boys were standing. It seemed that at least one had hit because they heard a loud swear word. The boys came out, looking confused. Simon's head was covered with mud, and Gimpy had mud splattered all over his school shirt. Beryl had saved one last mud pie, which she threw straight at Earnie, and it hit him on the shoulder with considerable force. The boys were so surprised to be attacked that they stood rooted to the spot while Beryl and Carol ran across the road and into the park, laughing and Nah-Nah-Nah-Nah-ing loudly.

After a short moment, the boys came to their senses, dropped their bags of grass, and began running after them. But instead of running down the path, Beryl and Carol ran into the nearby park, which they should have known was surrounded by a fence. Simon laughed. Obviously, the girls had made a huge mistake. They would be trapped.

The bullies, surprised at the girls' rookie blunder, followed them into the park shouting and sneering, "Idiots, we have you now!" and "We'll get you!"

Beryl and Carol ran, but the bullies were getting closer. Then, just as the boys were closing in on them, the two girls split apart and ran around two sides of a patch of grass. But the boys didn't stop. Stupid girls—they had just made another mistake that would just slow them down. The bullies charged straight ahead, as this was the quickest way, certain that they had the girls cornered.

Suddenly, they were knee-deep in mud, dirty water, and freshly cut grass. Gimpy stumbled and fell flat on his face, and the other two had their shoes stuck deep in gooey mud. Beryl and Carol didn't waste time. They rushed to the bushes and grabbed the sack of cut grass they had hidden earlier. Then they ran back and emptied the grass right over the boys' heads, making sure some went down their collars. Earnie was screaming with anger, Gimpy was lying in the puddle covered from head to toe in mud, and Simon was standing on one leg, trying to fish his shoe from the sludge.

"Take that!" shouted Beryl as she threw another clump of grass over Simon's head.

"And here's a special delivery from the Peril!" laughed Carol, dumping the last handful on the crying Earnie. Then they turned and ran, laughing so hard they almost split their sides, and they didn't stop until they reached school.

"Brilliant plan," laughed Beryl, tears streaming from her eyes.

"For sure!" Carol grinned with satisfaction. "I know all about mud balls from when I bombed your parents' house! And when I saw that hose pipe and the little puddle, I realised that we could turn it into a nice mud bath for the boys. And covering it with grass was the icing on the cake." She grinned at the pun.

Beryl picked up a long stick from the ground.

"Kneel, Carol," she commanded.

Carol knelt on one knee. Then Beryl gently dubbed each of

her shoulders with the stick and proclaimed with royal flair, "Arise, Dame Peril!"

Peril had never felt prouder.

Needless to say, none of the High-Street Gang appeared at school, but the two girls had big smiles on their faces all day. They felt a surge of confidence, as if they could conquer the world. After school, they skipped and giggled all the way home, acting out the boys' surprise and defeat again and again. It was just too good!

It was the next morning on their way to school that Beryl and Dame Peril received the shock nothing could have prepared them for, and their souls grew cold.

CHAPTER 8

There, standing outside Mrs. Ecclestone's front gate, stood a big 'For Sale' sign.

The girls were distraught. Mrs. Ecclestone had been there since forever. She had babysat them when they were little. She had taught them to read, to make paper boats and bake cupcakes, she had been a second mother when they needed a shoulder to cry on or an ear to talk to—her house was their house. The girls came and went as they pleased, and she was always happy to see them, ready with a hug and a slice of cake or mug of hot chocolate. Mrs. Ecclestone's backyard was their access to the river, and it was here that they had spent the long summer days by its bank. She would bring them juice and watermelon and paper for boats. If Mrs. Ecclestone moved, there would be no friendly home to retreat to, and they would not be able to get to the river. Worst of all, there would be no Mrs. Ecclestone. Carol burst into tears, and Beryl just looked at the ground and didn't say a word all the way to school.

School was awful. Beryl had flunked maths again, and Mr. Duffy sent a note to her mother asking her to come in for a chat. Carol had not done geography homework, which was highly unusual for her, and it just had to be that day that the teacher asked her to read it out. She had to lie and say that she had forgotten her book at home. The girls were miserable.

It was on their trek home that Beryl and Carol became aware

of what they had been seeing for a long time but had failed to notice. There were more and more 'For Sale' signs up around town, sometimes with pictures of smiling estate agents. The Joneses, Old Taffy, the Griffiths family, and even the corner shop all had signs posted outside. Some of them had 'SOLD' stickers stuck diagonally across them as if deserving a celebration. They knew all of these people! They were friends and acquaintances, and some of the families had kids their age who they had played with since kindergarten. Beryl and Carol were alarmed.

"What's happening to our town?" Beryl saw yet another sign outside the Roberts' home.

"I don't know, but I'm beginning to understand why my parents are arguing all the time." Carol looked at the pavement and fiddled with her bag awkwardly.

It was true. Carol's parents, who had always been happy, had been quarrelling a lot lately. They tried to hide it from her and Jerry, but they both heard snippets of conversations, as did Beryl next door. They knew it was something about work and Birmingham and commuting long distances, but until now, they could not piece it together. Something terrible was going on.

When the girls arrived home, they threw their bags over the fence of their houses and headed straight to Mrs. Ecclestone's. As always, she was wearing her rosy apron and was in the middle of baking something. She welcomed them with her cheerful face and warm smile, but they could tell it was an effort, and her eyes were red from crying. They sat down by the kitchen table as they had so many times before, munching chocolate cake which usually made them happy but now tasted bland. No one spoke for a long time.

Finally, Beryl looked up and asked, "What's going on, Mrs. E?"

Mrs. Ecclestone took her time to answer, searching for words and looking glum.

"I am so sorry, girls. I have to sell the house. There's nothing I can do. I've tried everything, but nothing has worked."

"But why?" begged Beryl. This was horrible news.

"It's what is happening all around," Mrs. Ecclestone sighed. "You know that I've worked at the textile factory for 27 years. Well, now things are becoming tough, and they have to fire many people, and the first to go are research and development staff, like me. So, I will be unemployed, and there is no other work to be found around here. At the same time, house prices in our area are going up. I simply can't afford to live here anymore. I'm going to have to move into my daughter's house in Bristol until I can find somewhere cheaper."

"Well, if everyone is moving out, why are house prices becoming more expensive? And why are workplaces closing down?" Beryl might have been bad at maths, but she had a keen sense of business.

"It's all about the London stock market, dear," Mrs. Ecclestone explained. "Stocks have been going up, and stockbrokers get huge Christmas bonuses, sometimes tens of thousands of pounds." The girls were astonished. They had never realised anyone could make that much money.

"When they have that much cash to spare, they look around for investments." Mrs. E cut another piece of cake. "One of their favourites is getting a second home in the country. They leave them empty for most of the year, and during the summer, they come for a holiday, to relax with the family, or do some fishing and sightseeing. A pretty little country town like ours in the gorgeous West of England, but just a few hours' drive from London, full of pretty houses, cobbled streets, and quaint shops, with the national park, rivers, and the Irish sea nearby, well, this is the perfect place for a country home.

"It is no problem for them to pay high prices. So many London stockbrokers have bought houses around here recently that prices have been driven way beyond our reach. Workplaces close, and people like me are forced to move out. As you know, the textile factory employs half the town in one way or another. If that closes, the result will be a ghost town."

This was awful news. It was unimaginable that their lovely little village would become a ghost town, full of London summer tourists, known locally as 'Grockles.' The three of them chewed their cake slowly, but they could hardly swallow. Mrs. E looked as though she was going to cry, so they just gave her a big hug, promised to come by tomorrow and made their way home. There was nothing to say.

The girls stood outside the front gate, not wanting to go inside. Suddenly Carol burst into tears.

"Beryl," she managed to mumble between sobs, "the textile factory is the main client of my mother's accounting firm. If they close down, so will my mother's firm. Now I understand what's going on with my parents. We'll have to sell the house and move to Birmingham."

CHAPTER 9

What Carol had feared turned out to be true. She found her mother sitting alone in her home office. When she told her about Mrs. E and asked her what was going on, Carol's mother had to confess.

"I am so sorry, darling." She held Carol's hands in hers. "Your father and I meant to tell you, but we held back because we're desperately trying to find a solution, though we haven't found one yet." She paused for a moment, squeezing Carol's hands tightly. "If we lose the textile factory, I won't have enough work to keep my firm going. I will have to let Flo and David go. And if we don't have both Dad's and my income, we can't afford to keep the house."

"But Mum." Carol was holding back her tears. "The house. Beryl! Our River…" She was lost for words.

"I know, darling. I know." Carol's mum, Naomi, wiped a tear away. She and her husband, Isaac, were both heartbroken by the situation. "We've lived here all your life, and your father and I love it here. This was our dream. And poor Jerry, just as he has been awarded school basketball captain, his lifelong dream. But the Textile factory is doing its very best to hang on, and anyway, nothing will happen till late next spring, which is the best time to sell. We could get a better price then. And meanwhile, we might find a solution. Dad is doing everything he can; he's been looking for a better position at other universities."

"Where would we go, Mum?" Carol was desperate.

"Maybe Birmingham. Houses are cheaper there. If we could get a good price for our house, we would be able to buy a nice place there. You might even like it."

Carol hated the thought. She despised cities. She loved her river and their little town, and most of all, she loved Beryl. How could she live without Beryl? Life would not be worth living. They had been inseparable since their two families had moved out of the city and bought the two adjoining cottages together. It had been such a bold and exciting step for their parents, and they never looked back. Carol had been four months old, and Beryl was just born. Stupid London stockbrokers!

Carol cried, and her mother hugged her until she calmed down. They talked for a long while, but they were going around in circles. Her mother promised that she and Dad would do all they could, but behind her shaky voice, she did not sound hopeful.

* * *

Later, the two friends sat on the riverbank, talking for hours and throwing small stones into the water.

Beryl, who was as desperate as Carol, asked, "Carol, how much money do your parents need to keep the house?"

"We owe the bank 20,000 pounds for the house. If we can pay that back in one lump sum, we'll own the house, and my mum won't have to work." Carol's eyes dropped to the ground.

"Wow, that's a huge sum!" Beryl gasped.

Carol's expression sunk even further, and she looked as though she was about to burst into tears again. Then, all of a sudden, the look on her face changed completely.

"Yes." She stood up and brushed her jeans. "It *is* a huge sum." She picked up one last rock and threw it as far as she could into the swirling waters. "And I'm going to find it."

Then she turned and walked home.

CHAPTER 10

C arol did not waste time. As soon as she got home, she went up to her room and began preparing noticeboard cards, each decorated with a flower, tree, or heart.

'Babysitter available. 12-year-old, caring and responsible girl, loves children.'

She thought about the 12-year-old for a while. Technically she was still 11, but she convinced herself that two months and 21 days was negligible.

'Car washing. I will make your car shine like never before.'

Yuck. Carol hated washing cars.

'Handy, hard-working girl. I will clean your house, weed your garden, do your shopping, walk your dog, or any other odd jobs around the house.'

Hmmm. Everything Carol avoided doing at home.

She made a few more signs, then began compiling a list of money-making schemes. A lemonade stand in town… Beryl and Carol had tried that when they were seven years old. They had stood in the main street from early morning and by the evening, had made only two pounds and seventy-one pence. Carol calculated that if they sold lemonade every day, it would take about nineteen years to make enough money for the house, and she only had till spring. Still, everything counted now. She compiled one of the well-known Carol lists:

1. Lemonade-stand
2. Baking birthday cakes for busy mums
3. Maths lessons for primary school kids
4. Ask at fish and chip shop
5. Ask at Ice cream shop
6. Ask at Pizza
7. Ask at the cinema
8.
9.
10.

Carol sat a while longer, racking her brain for fresh ideas to fill the last three slots. There was nothing more she could think of. She was prepared to do anything. The only principle was not to work for Mum and Dad, which would usually have been her first choice. No point in taking their money because they were all saving for the same thing.

There was one more thing she could do, but it filled her with dread. She would have to talk to Beryl about it, and Beryl would not be happy.

The next morning, on the way to school, Carol was excited to show Beryl her list and all the signs she had prepared. To her amazement, her friend was also clutching a bunch of cards. When they compared, it seemed they were almost identical. 'Make your car shine like new.' 'Walk your dog anytime.' 'Feed your cat when you're away.'

Carol was so touched she felt the tears welling up again but decided to hug Beryl instead. They agreed to hang up all the signs because Beryl claimed that having different phone numbers would create competition, and competition would generate business. The plan was to go around town after school, hanging them up.

But after school turned out to be a long and painful wait. Beryl had flunked the biology test, which was usually her best subject. She felt too ashamed to tell her parents about it. She knew she could handle the information, but she just had not seemed to have had the time and patience to study lately. Both girls had not finished their homework because of the previous evening's sign-making sessions. Not having done homework was old news for Beryl but new news for Carol. It seemed that being dubbed 'Peril' had had some effect on Carol. Her parents would not be pleased. The girls were glum but determined to hang the signs up around town anyway.

"Going anywhere?" Earnie said, his plump face stuffed with chewing gum and his shirt stained with chocolate. He and his two henchmen stood by the school gate, arms folded menacingly and blocking their way. Simon looked scary in his black shirt and pants, and Gimpy's cynical sneer was creepy. The High-Street Gang had not forgotten what the girls had done to them the other day and had sworn revenge.

Beryl and Carol stopped in their tracks, fearful. Usually, they would have retreated into school and waited for the boys to leave, as had happened so many times previously. That is what the three boys were expecting them to do, and they stood waiting for the girls' humiliation with mocking expressions on their smug faces. The two friends looked awkwardly at each other, uncertain of what to do next, and that old shameful feeling crept into their hearts.

But something had changed. The girls were not sure what that something was and did not wait to analyse it. But Beryl knew one thing, which she had learned from her dad. If you are going to fight, never fold your arms. She nodded at Carol, and then, suddenly and with no warning, she lunged at Gimpy, using her nails to scratch his bare arm. Carol hesitated for a split second, then followed her friend's lead. She rushed headlong between Simon and the injured Gimpy, who was holding his arm and screaming in pain. The girls busted through the blockade like two bulls through a paper fence and ran as fast as they could towards town. The other schoolkids saw what happened and burst out laughing and jeering. Neither the Gang nor the girls could believe what had just happened. But it had happened. Something *had* changed.

Something had changed for the bully boys, too. After their humiliating defeat, they sat in a deserted bus stop looking miserable. Earnie was chewing even more gum, Simon looked depressed, and Gimpy was smoking. They had planned to embarrass the two girls in front of the whole school, imagining this would earn them lots of points with their classmates. They badly needed these points because they had no friends other than themselves. Instead, they had been shown up in front of everyone and were now the laughingstock of their class.

They swore revenge. But dealing with both girls together was not working out well. They would catch them one at a time and show them who was boss. The boys began to plan.

CHAPTER 11

On Saturday morning, the two friends set off early carrying two rucksacks full of goodies, carefully packed according to Carol's list. Beryl and Carol had told their parents that they were going for an all-day picnic in the park, which was a half-truth and half-lie, depending on which park you meant. Of course, their parents didn't mind at all. A day with fewer kids at home meant peace and quiet for them. The girls had been careful to sit in the park for a while until some passers-by saw them ('Our Alibi,' Carol called it). Then they quietly snuck towards the forest, making sure no one saw or followed them.

Entering the woods again was as scary as the first time less than a week ago. After a few minutes into the forest, the girls felt the same chill and fear grab them. They stopped and looked at each other with horror.

"What are we thinking?" Carol whispered, afraid someone might hear her. "We must be crazy coming back in here. Let's go home."

Beryl was thinking the same thing. The dark forest, the thick bushes, and the creepy noises made her shudder.

"I know," she muttered, unsure of what to do. "Maybe we should turn back?"

"Beryl, you know this place is full of murders and kidnappers and criminals. We should have our heads examined coming in here. Think of what happened to Tim. We don't want to end up like him!"

Fifteen years ago, back in 1982 and long before the girls were born, Tim Marston, who had been 17 years old at the time, had walked into these woods but had never come back. There were police and search parties; it was all over the news, but what happened to Tim remained a mystery. Some said he was kidnapped or murdered, others thought there had been an accident or he had drowned in the river, or perhaps a wild animal had got him. But as the body was never found, no one could say for sure. It was since then that the forest had become 'forbidden.' Even adults kept away, claiming that they did not want to set a bad example for their kids, but the truth was that the stories had grown larger than life, and people were afraid. Everyone knew the old men's tales of the forest being a hiding place for smugglers and criminals. After Tim's disappearance, these stories were justified. And now, even discussing 'the disappearance' had become forbidden.

The girls stood still for a while, thinking about what might have happened to Tim.

Then Beryl said, "Carol, if we don't go now, we never will. If we chicken out now, we'll always be chickens. Think of our beautiful secret garden. Let's do it."

Carol thought for a while, then nodded. Beryl was right. If you chicken out once, you will probably chicken out again. And besides, she was dying to see the clearing again. They gave each other a timid fist bump and carried on in the forest.

After a while, they found the path they had walked down and followed the markings in the trees. They arrived at the clearing in just under 45 minutes. The moment they saw it, all their fear melted away. They were home!

Beryl laid back on the grass, her head on a rucksack pillow, chewing a twig and looking up at the giant oak canopy. From below, it seemed even grander, a vast dome sheltering and protecting them.

"This is just too good," she murmured. "I can't think of anything that would make it better."

Carol laughed.

"I can," she said. "How about your mum's cheesecake?"

"Now you're talking." Beryl rummaged in her rucksack and pulled out two large slices of her mother's best cake, wrapped in red and white napkins. "Here you go," she said, passing Carol what she thought was the smaller piece. Then she changed her mind and gave her friend the bigger one. Carol pretended not to notice but smiled to herself.

The girls munched their cake slowly and deliberately, savouring every bite. This was the perfect picnic.

It was a gorgeous spring day. Beryl and Carol explored the area more thoroughly than on their first rushed visit, and it was even more beautiful than they remembered. The sun shone through the trees, speckling their garden in light. The trees surrounding the clearing rose like a giant fence, shielding them from the outside world. It was just perfect. They had wanted to play ball but didn't like the idea of crushing flowers. So, they played Frisbee for a while, then sat down under the oak to eat their picnic and read their favourite book, *The Wind in The Willows*.

After eating and reading, they shared a cup of tea from their thermos and discussed where to keep the things they wanted to leave in their magic garden.

"Dig a hole," suggested Beryl.

"No," said Carol. "It would rot, get wet, or animals would get to it. Better we hang one rucksack in a tree."

"Great idea," Beryl nodded. "How about building a small place for a fire, where we can boil water for tea and cook potatoes and sausages?"

"Excellent idea!" Carol was enthusiastic. "We could build it there." She pointed at a bald patch near the river. "We can lay some stones around and have a pile of wood nearby."

The girls were excited. Their minds were spinning with possibilities.

"Where would we keep the milk and food?" Carol looked around.

Beryl thought for a while. "We could rig up a fridge by tying a canvas bag to a tree root and hanging it in the river so that our milk and other perishable foods were kept nice and cold." She was pleased with her idea and looked at Carol for approval.

Carol nodded vaguely but was not listening. She had that dreamy expression, her eyes glazed over as though she was looking far, far away.

"What?" Beryl prodded her shoulder. "Where have you flown off to now, Nonco?"

Carol was quiet for a long moment, and then she said softly, "Beryl, we are going to build a house."

CHAPTER 12

There was nothing else the girls could think or talk of. They dreamt the house, discussed the house, planned the house, drew the house. It filled their days, it filled their nights, it filled their hearts and minds. The house. Their house!

After school, they spent a few hours in the library studying basic architecture and looking at pictures of wooden cabins. Eventually, they spent so much time there that Beryl's mum became suspicious.

"What are you doing in the library all day, every day?" Mum shot Beryl her suspicious look.

"Studying Architecture." Beryl smiled sweetly. There was no point in lying when you could tell the truth.

"Are you planning on building a house?" Beryl's mum asked.

"Sure, Mum, of course we are! We'll be moving out before you know it."

"Thank heavens, some peace at last." Mum grinned, and that was that. Truth was the best lie!

The girls worked from Beryl's room. They became quite skillful at reading and drawing house plans, using special graph paper, sharp pencils, and a square ruler. As usual, Sam, Beryl's little brother, was a problem. He smelt something was up and kept creeping up to the door and eavesdropping so that the girls had to talk in whispers and occasionally shoo him away with threats and bribes.

Despite the obstacles, the house plans gradually took shape. It would have one large room, which would be divided into a living room, kitchen corner, and bedroom—in case they ever got to sleep there, though they could not work out how that would ever happen. Most importantly, there would be a cute little porch looking onto their garden.

Of course, the structural details had to be planned, too. The girls needed to learn how to work with wood, so Beryl dropped art lessons, and Carol dumped ballet (what a relief!). Instead, they joined the carpentry class, which amazed their mothers, though Beryl's dad, who was an avid amateur carpenter, was delighted. He offered to help, and together they practised sawing and screwing and hammering and making a variety of woodworking joints, and after a few weeks, their carpentry teacher, who was just the French teacher filling in, announced that the two girls knew more than he did. Beryl's little brother, Sam, was jealous.

"Girls shouldn't be doing carpentry," he muttered one day, but Beryl's dad pointed out that their work was a lot better than that of any boy he knew, so Sam reluctantly shut up and sulked away. Beryl and Carol felt really proud of themselves. It was great to be good at something girls were not supposed to be good at.

For their end-of-term Carpentry project, the girls built a large box that was also a bench. It had hinges for the lid and a sturdy clasp to put a lock in. When it was finished, Beryl's dad picked it up and was delighted to hear from the carpentry tutor that the girls had done 'Class A work.' The bully boys stared in disbelief when they saw the box being loaded into the car. They found it difficult to believe that 'stupid girls' could build something so remarkable. When the girls got home, Carol's mother gave them two green cushions to put on top, so it was the perfect seat and storage!

"It's absolutely stonking!" Beryl admired their work.

With the help of Beryl's dad, they completed their home project, a kitchen table built from new pine, with big square legs and a thick surface. When they had painted on the final coat of varnish, Beryl's family stood in the backyard, admiring their handiwork, and Carol's mum looked on from over the fence. Everyone clapped, even Sam. It looked so well built, and the bench box fitted under the table perfectly, just as they had planned.

"What will you do with all this nice furniture you've built?" asked Beryl's dad.

"Oh, we don't know," said Carol. "Maybe we'll give it to the Girl Guides' clubhouse." Beryl's dad nodded in approval, but both girls looked at the ground. Beryl wished she had a big moustache to hide her smile, and Carol developed a sudden sneezing fit, trying not to laugh. They knew exactly what they were going to do with their furniture.

But the next day, when they came home from school, a gloomy black cloud shaded their joy. On the sign outside Mrs. Ecclestone's was a diagonal sticker gaily declaring: 'SOLD.' Mrs. E had left. Carol's mother explained that she was too brokenhearted to say goodbye to the girls. She left a chocolate cake with white icing saying:

With much love always. Mrs. E.

CHAPTER 13

It was now mid-April. Over the last weeks, the girls had been collecting wood, old furniture, metal sheets, and any other bits and pieces they could find. They searched in skips, rubbish dumps, work yards, and backyards. Suddenly everything seemed useful, stuff they would have previously considered rubbish. 'One man's trash is another girl's treasure,' they chorused as they searched.

They found quite a few pieces of wood. Plywood sheets for the walls, two old windows (one with the glass still in it!), a kitchen door, a large tarpaulin (suitable for the floor), bits and pieces of metal, hooks and hinges, a door handle with a knocker, a blow-up mattress, and an old kettle you could stand on a fire. Of course, Carol had kept lists of everything. The only items they had to pay for were ten six two-by-fours wooden posts from the hardware store necessary to build the frame with, which they carried home two at a time while their parents were at work. They smuggled all their treasures to the back of Mrs. Ecclestone's house, which now stood sad and empty, and hid everything behind the garden shed.

Now the two friends were sitting in their clearing, discussing the house and how to build it. It was a beautiful spring day, and they had been dipping in the river. The water was still cold, so they made a fire and covered themselves in blankets they had 'borrowed' from Carol's mum. On top of the fireplace stood their old kettle, black and nearly boiling. All that Brownies knowledge was coming in handy.

Every time they visited, the girls had carried some useful things: bits of wood, tools, pots and pans, cutlery, books, and games. They had built a little shelf from stones and planks under the giant oak, where they arranged all their possessions.

The house plans were ready, and Beryl and Carol knew precisely where and how they would build it. They could picture the house in their mind, nestling under the oak's canopy, half-protected by its branches, but with a porch exposed to the warm sun with a roof for rainy days. Carol had drawn a picture of how it would look (during a music lesson), and they hung it from the tree above the shelf. Everything was in place to get going except for two major problems.

The first was that they had no idea how to get all the heavy stuff to the forest, and the second was that they did not have enough wood for the roof. They had racked their brains and could not come up with an answer. The table and box seat, the door, and the windows were just too big to carry into the forest. They sat under the willow, watching their river as it danced downstream, discussing the problem, but no answers came to mind. They thought of carrying the load on Sam's trolley, but its wheels would get stuck in the rough forest ground, and, of course, people would notice them. They thought of bringing the pieces bit by bit at night, but that was out of the question. In desperation, Beryl suggested building a helicopter, but Carol pulled a face, and the joke was over.

Carol poured some tea, and Beryl cut some of her mum's carrot cake (probably the best carrot cake in the Northern Hemisphere, she had said, because she was not sure if there was carrot cake in the Southern Hemisphere).

"I give up. Let's leave it for another day," Beryl shrugged. Carol had given up as well, so she picked up TWITW and opened where they had left off some time ago.

"Hullo, Mole!" said the Water Rat.

"Hullo, Rat!" said the Mole.

"This has been a wonderful day!" said the Mole […] "Do you know, I've never been in a boat before in all my life."

"What?" cried the Rat, open-mouthed: "Never been in a—you never—well I—what have you been doing, then?"

"Is it so nice as all that?" asked the Mole shyly, though he was quite prepared to believe it as he leant back in his seat and surveyed the cushions, the oars, the rowlocks, and all the fascinating fittings, and felt the boat sway lightly under him.

"Nice? It's the only thing." Beryl and Carol quoted as if one person. "Believe me, my young friend, there is nothing—absolutely nothing— half so much worth doing as simply messing about in boats. Simply messing."

By this time, both girls had stopped reading and just stared at each other, big smiles spreading over their faces, dreamy looks in their eyes.

They were going to build a boat.

CHAPTER 14

The boat was not going to be a boat exactly. It was too difficult to build a proper yacht, and there was no need for masts, sails, a rudder, or an engine. Its primary function would be to carry their stuff up the river, and so it would be a raft.

It did not take the girls long to plan it. They huddled together in the library, sifting through a large pile of boat books that Mrs. Norman, the librarian, had kindly assembled for them. There were loads of plans, so they chose the easiest ones, then picked the best bits out of each, and came up with their own version. They would take two long logs from the forest, clean them up, and then connect them with a row of planks to make a deck. The front bit (the bow, said Beryl) would be pointier than the back bit (the aft, said Carol). Finally, they would need to attach Styrofoam to the bottom to make the raft float even under a heavy load. Carol wanted a mast and sail, but Beryl said that it was a stupid idea because there was not enough wind. They argued about it for a while and decided not to decide.

The girls got to work the next day, sawing the planks in the backyard. Their parents were used to the woodwork factory in the backyard, so no one bothered them, except for once, when Beryl's mum came out to see if they wanted tea.

"What are you two building now?" she inquired.

And they replied, *"Oh, messing about, simply messing about,"* careful to leave the boat word out of the sentence.

Once the planks were ready, they moved to behind Mrs. E's house. Carol, lover of lists, kept a running tally of their work:

Saturday:

Saw long planks into 9 shorter pieces	1.5 hours
Find two logs	1 Hour 15 minutes
Drag logs to behind Mrs. E.'s shed	30 minutes
Clean logs up	1.5 hours
Screw planks onto logs	1.5 hours

It was a long, hard day, but by the end of it, there was a finished looking raft lying behind Mrs. E's garden shed. Both girls stood admiring it, beaming at each other and at themselves. It looked just right! But evening was upon them, and it was time to go, so they covered the raft with branches and set off home.

"I wish we could sail it right now," said Beryl as they walked down the path.

"You'd sail to the bottom of the river, Nonco," Carol laughed.

* * *

The next morning, they woke earlier than usual for a Sunday, had a quick breakfast, and got back to work. This is how Carol's list looked:

Sunday:

Washing Dads' cars for £5 each	1.5 hours
Robbing our own piggy banks (Carol £7.90 and Beryl £6.21)	3 minutes
Going to the DIY store to buy Styrofoam, glue, rope, and Bungee cords for £19.95	45 minutes
Eating ice cream with leftover money (B: Choc, C: Vanilla Strawberry)	30 minutes
Smuggling Styrofoam past families	One tense hour
Glueing Styrofoam to bottom of raft	1.5 hours

And that was it! Their raft was ready.

"We need a name." Beryl looked at the raft as though it was a baby.

"I've been thinking of that." Carol looked smug. "How about the Kon-Tiki?"

They both loved the Kon-Tiki book, all about a Norwegian explorer called Thor Heyerdahl, who had sailed a simple raft from South America to the Polynesian islands. He had travelled a distance of 4,300 miles just to show that the ancient South American people had migrated that way.

"Good idea," said Beryl, "but that name's already taken. How about the Kon-Taki?"

"Kon-Tiki, Kon-Taki." Carol played with the sounds. "Kon-Taki it is, and we shall break a bottle of champagne over its bow to name it!"

"Absolutely!" Beryl jumped up. "Let me see what I can 'borrow' from my mum, she likes a good glass of champagne, and I think I saw a bottle somewhere." Beryl ran home while Carol tidied up the tools.

15 minutes later, Beryl returned. "I've got good news and bad

news," she announced.

"Give me the bad," said Carol, disappointed.

"No champagne," said Beryl.

Carol was not surprised. Beryl's mum would never leave a good bottle of champagne lying around for too long.

"Give me the good," she grinned.

"I've got something bubbly."

"What's bubbly that isn't champagne?"

"Fanta."

"That's fanta-stic," laughed Carol.

"No need to fant about it," Beryl echoed.

"Don't be an in-fant," replied Carol.

"Fantabulous!" Beryl countered.

Once they finished going over every Fanta pun they could think of, they stood by the bow of their new raft. Beryl put the Fanta in a plastic bag, they both held the edge of the bottle together and with a 'one, two, three,' brought it down on the bow. Nothing happened.

"Harder, Nonco!" said Carol.

"Okay, okay, let's go again." Beryl gritted her teeth and brought the bottle down hard.

This time the bottle shattered into tiny fragments, the over-excited Fanta whooshing all over the bag. It was an appropriate explosion.

"We now name this vessel the HMS Kon-Taki," announced Beryl.

Carol did a little jig and chanted, "Three cheers and hip hip hooray!"

CHAPTER 15

Beryl and Carol's search for jobs was not going well. The cinema, pizza hut, and the ice cream shop all had enough workers. 'Don't call us, we'll call you, thank you very much.' It appeared that quite a few other kids were eager for work. People were losing jobs, money was scarce, and you could feel the gloom around town as 'For Sale' signs sprouted like mushrooms after the rain. To make things worse, gangs of happy Grockles from London began visiting, laughing noisily, bargaining over cheap souvenirs, and acting as if they already owned the town. So far, the only hope for a job was one phone call to Beryl enquiring about babysitting, which ended with 'Thank you, dear, you seem most appropriate. I will most certainly call you if my husband ever agrees to take me out.' Carol had landed a once-a-week maths lesson with an irritating seven-year-old boy. While she was teaching him, she calculated that at this rate, it would take 108 years to get the money she needed for her parents to keep the house.

The couple who had bought Mrs. E's house came to visit one weekend and looked around. They left without even introducing themselves, which no country person would ever dream of doing. At least this meant that the girls could use Mrs. E's backyard as a base.

When Carol's family sat down to dinner that evening, her father announced, "I have some news. I managed to find a job teaching at Cambridge University."

Carol and Jerry stopped chewing mid-bite. Carol's mother stared at her knife and fork. She had obviously been dreading this moment.

"W...what? Dad?" Carol stuttered. "You...you'll be moving without us?"

"It's just temporary, darling. It's good news, really." Mum didn't sound convincing. "You see, if Dad moves to Cambridge, he will earn much more, and that means we can hang on here till next spring and hope the textile factory sorts out. House prices will be higher by then, so we can buy a better house in Birmingham and that'll be closer to Dad, and later on, he can move back with us. If Dad doesn't take the job, we'll have to move this summer."

No one said a word after that. The clinking of cutlery and plates sounded like church bells at a funeral. It was down to either leaving their beloved house and town in two months or being separated from Dad. There was no third choice. Carol wanted to run away to her room, but she knew it would upset her parents, and they were upset enough already.

After dinner, Carol and her dad sat on the porch together. Carol adored her father. He was a university professor teaching philosophy of science. He knew so much, and he knew how to make this knowledge exciting and funny at the same time. Carol loved the way he could weave a web of science, poetry, history, philosophy, and jokes. The news that he might have to move away was unbearable.

"Don't worry, my love, it'll all pan out. I don't have to go before August, and I know we can sort this out before too long." Dad sucked deeply on his empty pipe. He had long given up lighting it.

"But, Dad, I can't live in a smelly city without you and Beryl and the river...my life would be over!"

"You can visit me in squeaky clean Cambridge." Dad tried to joke it off. But she could tell he was feeling down. "Cambridge is too expensive for us, but if we do sell and move to Birmingham, we might have money left over, so I can move back with our family after a while."

Carol lay awake for hours. She imagined the horror of being trapped in a small flat with her mother and Jerry, with no nature apart from parks full of noisy kids on swings and rowdy drunk people coming out of pubs at night. And no Beryl! The thought of life without her father, her best friend, the river, and her little town was awful. But moving to Birmingham was the only way their family could eventually be together. There was no way Carol wanted to see her parents live separately. She loved her family as it was! Carol was torn and confused. The more she thought about it, the more horrific it seemed, so after a while, she switched tracks and began thinking about money-making schemes instead. Carol was determined to find a way to keep their house. But she could come up with no new ideas.

* * *

It was only the raft that kept the girls' hopes afloat on the gloomy seas of despair. They discussed how to stack all the stuff they had collected, how to pull it upriver—this would not be easy! But there would be no rafting until Wednesday. Carol had swimming and Beryl basketball, Tuesday was Woodwork and getting ready for the dreaded end of term Maths test.

"Ugh!" groaned Carol. "I forgot about that. I don't know anything!"

"You're kidding me," sighed Beryl, her heart sinking as she remembered the exam. "Your 'I don't know anything' is my excellent."

But the real test would come on Wednesday. Would the Kon-Taki float or sink? And could she carry all their heavy stuff to the clearing?

CHAPTER 16

Finally, Wednesday afternoon arrived. The dreaded end-of-term maths exam was over, and both girls felt they had just scraped by ('Barely,' said Beryl, 'Hardly,' moaned Carol). The clocks had sprung forward, and daylight was now stretching into the evening, so they were free to enjoy a long afternoon. They ran home, stuffed lunch down their throats, told their mums they were going to finish some woodwork in the back, put on swimsuits under their clothes, and snuck their wellies out in plastic bags. Then, creeping low behind the bushes, they carried all the pieces of wood, furniture, metal, and tools from Mrs. E's backyard to the edge of the forest. Once everything was behind the trees, it was much easier to carry their stuff further upriver to where HMS Kon-Taki lay waiting for its maiden voyage.

Beryl and Carol dragged their large seat-box to where the raft lay just a few metres from the riverbank. They placed it in the middle of the raft and fastened it on with the bungee cords they had bought at the hardware store. Beryl tied a rope to the bow.

It was time to get wet. The girls took off their top clothes, pulled on their wellies, and waded into the river, gasping as the freezing water squeezed their breath. They grabbed hold of the rope and began tugging, but the raft did not budge—it was way too heavy.

"Oh, no!" Carol looked worried. "I hope it floats!"

"Only one way to find out, Nonco." Beryl yanked the rope

harder. The raft lurched towards the water, groaning, scrapping, and bouncing over stones and roots and getting stuck under its heavy load. Finally, after much pulling and pushing, it stood poised by the river, nose halfway in and backside halfway out.

"Let's go! Gently does it, lads." Carol lent back, grasping the rope in both hands and pulling.

"Aye, aye, Captain Peril," mimicked Beryl. "Gently does it!"

The girls grimaced and heaved, and 30 seconds later, the bow of the Kon-Taki hit the water for the first time.

It went under.

"Keep pulling, keep pulling!" urged Beryl. "We need to get the part with the Styrofoam in." The two friends pulled with all their might, and a minute later, the raft was completely submerged. It rocked back and forth frantically, water spilling over its deck as it went below the surface. The girls looked on with panic, certain it was going to sink to the bottom. But a few seconds later, the raft bobbed up defiantly and steadied itself, seemingly happy, like a fish that had been returned to the water. It was in its natural home, and it liked it! Beryl and Carol were pleased. Very pleased!

"And so, she floats!" Beryl high-fived Carol.

"Float, she does!" Carol hi-fived back. "Even with that heavy box. If she can carry that, she can carry us."

They stood in the water admiring their raft as it swayed on the river's currents until Carol splashed Beryl's face and quickly escaped out of the water. "Let's get to work."

"Start passing me stuff, Nonco!" grinned Beryl, wiping the water off her face. Carol handed her the larger items first: the door, windows, pieces of wood, metal thingies, and then pots, pans, and the lighter stuff. Beryl stacked these inside the box, making sure everything was well balanced. The raft was much heavier now, and water was once again spilling over its deck.

"That's as much as she can take, methinks, laddie." Beryl put on her sailor voice again. They stopped packing, and Carol waded back into the water. She grabbed the rope and began towing the raft upriver while Beryl stood aft and pushed, trying to keep the raft stable. Moving forward was not easy, but it was moving! They made their way slowly upstream, watchful not to slip on riverbed rocks. After fifty minutes of shoving, pulling, balancing, and slipping, the Kon-Taki was at the clearing with house gear intact. The girls' wellies were full of mud, water, and probably fish, and they were shivering from cold, but they could not have cared less—their plan had worked!

CHAPTER 17

H alf an hour later, Beryl and Carol sat huddled around the
fire, covered in blankets and trying to soak some warmth
into their shivering bones. Each held a cup of watery hot
chocolate between their two shaking hands. Scattered around them
were piles of wood and metal, plastic sheets, pots and pans, tools,
and folders with house plans, all retrieved from the Kon-Taki. In the
centre was their pride and joy, the seat-box topped with two green
cushions. The Kon-Taki itself was tied to a root and seemed much
happier now that its burden had been lifted. It bounced gaily on
the flowing waters, bobbing up and down as if it were enjoying its
mission in life for the first time.

The girls were cold and exhausted from packing and unpack-
ing all their possessions and pulling the boat upriver. But they had
made a giant step forward. Around them was all they needed to
start building a house. They reckoned that one more raft trip upriver
would be enough. After a rest, the two friends pulled themselves up
stiffly and began to organise their possessions.

When they had finished, everything was neatly stacked around
the oak tree and in the seat-box. Their mothers would have been
impressed; it looked nothing like their messy bedrooms. The beautiful
glade felt like home. All that was missing was a house, and building
their home was going to be fun! Best of all, Easter holidays were
around the corner—three school-free weeks to build the house in.

The girls had time for a quick game before heading home, so they chose their favourite, backgammon.

"Be prepared to lose, Nonco!" Carol made her opening attack.

"Not on your life. I'm going to flatten you!" Beryl threw the dice and made her counterattack.

After a few moves, it looked as though Carol's well-planned assault would win her the match, but Beryl made a crazy move, and it paid off. She managed to turn the game around and win. That was the fun thing about backgammon. It was fast and exciting and quickly switched one way or the other.

When they finished playing, Beryl stood up and declared, "Okay, Captain Carol, let's do it." Of course, she did not think for one minute that Carol was Captain, but she liked the way it sounded.

Naturally, Carol did not object.

It was the moment they had been thinking about all day. They would try to sail the Kon-Taki home. Could their little boat do it? Could it carry them both, or would it sink or crash into the riverbank? How long would it take? Would they get wet? They hoped that this would be a faster way home than the hour-long walk through the forest.

They untied the Kon-Taki from its moorings. Beryl stood on the bank and held the raft steady while Carol crawled on. The Kon-Taki swayed backwards and forwards, bucking like a bronco and almost throwing Carol into the river, but eventually, it stabilised and accepted its rider. Carol picked up one of the broomstick oars they had stowed on the raft. She stuck one side into the bank and held the other, keeping the raft steady while Beryl climbed on. The girls placed themselves in the centre, holding on to each other. The Kon-Taki rocked but didn't sink! It was time to launch.

"State precise time, First Mate?" Carol took command.

"18:07, Captain." Beryl put on her sailor's voice.

Carol pushed her stick against the riverbank, and the Kon-Taki lurched into the river and was swept away on its swirling currents. It rocked up and down and rolled from side to side as if undecided about the trip, but then relaxed and began heading downstream, gaining speed as it settled into the currents. The donkey had transformed into a racehorse—it seemed to relish the journey, hurtling down the river, steady and safe, knowing exactly what to do. Only occasionally did the girls have to push themselves away from the riverbank with the broomsticks. Once, the raft lurched sideways, and Carol nearly fell in and had to grab onto Beryl. But mostly they were hardly getting wet. It was a fantastic ride, better than any funfair. The girls were shrieking with joy, enjoying the speed and the excitement of their trip home. Before they knew it, they were at the last bend in the river, after which was Mrs. E's house.

"Slow down," Captain Carol commanded, sticking her broomstick in the riverbed.

"Aye aye, Captain." Beryl did the same. The raft slowed, rocked sideways, then came to a stop just before the last bend, after which they might be seen. They pushed and pulled with the broomsticks until Beryl caught a branch and hauled them in. They were home!

"Time, First Mate?" Carol asked.

Beryl looked at her watch. Then she looked at Carol with a sparkle in her eyes.

"18:18, Captain."

They had made it from the clearing to their houses in 11 minutes. It felt as though they had just broken the Olympic world record! Yes, it would take them over 45 minutes to drag the boat upriver, but they would have an expressway home when they needed it.

They were on top of the world.

CHAPTER 18

It was early Saturday afternoon. Because of chores and rain, the two girls arrived at the clearing later than they had planned. But now the sun was out, and for the last two hours, they had been digging holes in the damp earth for the house frame.

"Come and look at this!" Carol was clearing away a small pile of stones when her trowel hit something metallic, half-buried in the earth.

Beryl left the hole she was digging and came over, peering over Carol's shoulder.

Carol cleared some more soil and stones. They could now see the top of an old tobacco tin, with the faint yellow words 'Golden Virginia' printed on the faded green cover. Beryl recognised it from when her dad used to smoke—she had hated the smell but loved the tins.

Carol cleared more earth around the tin until it was finally free. She picked it up, and the girls took it to the log under the willow tree for closer inspection. She gave the can a shake. Something was rattling inside, something light. She tried to pull the lid off, but it was rusty and stuck.

"Hang on." Beryl went to their toolbox and returned with a screwdriver. "Try to prize it open."

Carol took the screwdriver and started working the lid off the tin. Bit by bit, she managed to pull the rusty edges away until the cover came loose. She pulled it off, and they both peered into the open tin. Inside lay a plastic bag containing a folded piece of paper. Slowly, so as not to damage anything, Carol unwrapped the bag and pulled it out. She unfolded the paper and laid it on the table. It was a letter, written on two sheets of standard school paper in blue pen. The words were faded, but they could still make them out. The first thing they noticed was the name at the bottom. In clear, bold letters, it said: '*Tim Marston*,' followed by a scrawled signature.

The girls were in shock. They looked at each other wide-eyed and then looked back at the paper to make sure it was true. Beryl whispered, "My God!" and Carol could only nod.

Tim Marston was the reason nobody came into the forest, even though the tragedy had happened way back in 1982, long before the girls were born. Tim had told his parents he was going hiking in the forest and had never returned. No one ever found out what had happened, and his body was never found. The girls often thanked him in their hearts because it meant people were scared of the forest, so their house remained a secret. At the same time, they realised it was a terrible tragedy, especially for Tim's parents.

Carol read out loud, with a slight tremble in her voice.

"February 18, 1982.

"To whoever finds this letter,

"My name is Tim Marston, and I am 17 years old. I have lived here all my life and have been visiting this clearing since I discovered it five years ago. No one else knows about it. Everybody thinks it's dangerous, and access is difficult. So if you found it—congratulations! This is the best place in the world."

Carol and Beryl both nodded in agreement, pleased that someone else knew how special their magic garden was. They were also relieved to hear Tim thought it was challenging to find. Carol continued reading.

"I am writing this note because I am about to run away—forever. I am going to join the Navy.

"I was adopted at the age of three from an orphanage, and I never found my birth parents. My adoptive parents, Mark and Rita, have always been very good to me, but they are old, and I was their only child, so they never really understood me. We tried to get on as a family, but it never worked—we argued too much, mainly about my future.

"All my life, I have loved the sea and wanted to be an explorer, just like my hero, Sir Ernest Shackleton, who was a great leader and adventurer and one of the first people to explore the Antarctic. That is

my only dream. But my parents won't hear anything about it. They want me to go to university, and worse, they want me to be a dentist, so I can work in their clinic and take it over after they retire. There is no way I am doing that!

"They won't let me go, and so I have no choice but to run away. It is time for me to make my own destiny. My parents cannot know, or they will find me and bring me back, so I will just vanish. To-morrow, I will take the train to Her Majesty's Naval Base in Portsmouth, where I will join the Navy. Next week is my 18th birthday, so I believe the Navy will let me join. This will be the most important moment of my life!

"If you find this, please tell my parents I am very, very sorry. I have thought and talked about nothing else for the last few years, but they did not hear me and could not understand, so I have no choice. I love them dearly and thank them for bringing me up and giving me all I need. I wish them only good things. Once I am established in the Navy, I will contact them, and I hope they will forgive me. If you find this letter, please give it to them, but not before I am gone for one year, which will be February 1983.

"Mark and Rita—you are my real Mum and Dad. I know you discouraged me from meeting my birth parents, but it is something I need to do. Now that I am 18, I will try to find them. I don't know my Dad's name, but I found my birth certificate. My mother was Julia Parker. I have not been able to find her yet.

"Dear Mark and Rita—Dad and Mum. I love you. I am sorry, but I hope to be happy at sea and make you proud.

"Tim Marston."

The girls were silent for a long, long time. Each tried to open her mouth to talk but then thought better and shut it again. They simply did not know what to say.

After several gaping attempts, Beryl managed to murmur some kind of 'No way,' and Carol 'no-way'd' her back, which broke the silence.

"My God," Beryl whispered. "Astonishing!"

Carol nodded. "That solves the mystery."

"Poor Tim." Beryl was sad. "Poor Tim's parents. Not knowing what happened to him all these years and thinking he was dead."

The girls sat silently, deep in thought.

"Why didn't he contact them again?"

"I don't know. Perhaps Tim decided he didn't want to see them or was worried about them being upset with him running away."

"Or he didn't want to be a dentist."

"Hey, what's on the second piece of paper?"

Carol unfolded the faded paper. It was a short note that looked as though it had been added later.

Carol read again.

"One more thing. During the last five years, I have read about, researched, and explored this forest. I know every path, tree, river, and cave in this area. From my study and investigations, I believe there is a treasure hidden nearby, perhaps by the falls, but my friends and I have not been able to find it. Maybe someone smaller than us will.

"When I come back one day, I will start searching for it again but, just in case I don't—well, it's up to you, whoever you are, and if you can find it, you deserve it. But I want a cut!

"Thanks."

"Wow, we could do with a treasure." Carol was excited.

"For sure. But so little to go on. Which falls? None around here that I know of. He mentions friends, but who could that be?"

"No idea. Maybe it's all fantasy," Carol mumbled.

But Beryl could see her friend was thinking about it. After a moment she asked her, "What do we do now?"

"I don't know." Suddenly Carol looked depressed. Because she did know. Then, with great difficulty, she blurted out. "We have to tell Tim's parents."

"If we tell them, we lose our clearing, and we will never build the house." Beryl was wringing her hands anxiously. "We'll have to give them the note, they'll want to see the clearing, and next thing you know, everyone and their uncle will come here, newspapers and all. Maybe we should just keep it to ourselves, and no one will ever know. This was so long ago!"

Carol put her face in her hands. Finally, she looked at Beryl.

"We could hide it, but we both know we wouldn't. Tim asked us to tell his parents. And they must know. It's the only right thing to do."

Beryl knew her friend was right. It was thanks to Tim that no one ever went into the forest, but now it would be thanks to Tim that the whole world would come. Her whole being did not want to tell anyone, but she knew they couldn't leave poor Tim's parents in the misery of believing their son was dead, which was just too awful.

Losing their secret garden was a terrible thought. A tear dropped from Carol's eye, and she noticed Beryl rubbing her eyes too.

The shadows were growing long, telling them it was time to head home.

Beryl stood up. "I don't even know where Tim's parents live."

"Let's ask some older people in town. Maybe Mrs. Norman. We'll have to clear our stuff out of this place before the party begins." Carol checked around to make sure all their gear was safely stored.

"Perhaps we can say we found the letter somewhere else?" Beryl tried one more time.

"Right, like where? Just in the middle of the forest? He mentions the clearing in his note. People would want to see it…"

The girls hugged for a long time, both crying. They took one last look at their beautiful garden, at the stuff they had brought to build the house, at their little raft bobbing on the water. Then they turned and walked away. The dream was over.

CHAPTER 19

"Are we sure we're doing the right thing?" Carol drummed her fingers on their office park bench. Beryl didn't reply— she had already asked Carol the same question three times that day. They both knew the answer but could not believe that they would have to give up their beloved clearing. But there was no question about what was right in this situation. The Marstons had to be told. And once they were told, everyone would know, and the next thing the clearing would be a public park and the forest a free-for-all.

After a long silence, Carol said, "Let's get this over with. We need to find out where Tim's parents live. But we have to get all our stuff out of the clearing before we tell them."

"Okay," mumbled Beryl meekly. "Are we going to throw it all away?"

"Yes. Or hide it. If we don't, our parents will find out where we have been all this time, and we will be terminated. We can't leave a trace. Maybe we should just put the letter in the post, so they don't know it's us. But who do we post it to, and who would show them Tim's clearing, and how did we find the letter? Anyway, there will be search parties." It all seemed so complicated.

An old lady with a little boy and a poodle on a leash ambled down the nearby path. The boy was wearing a sailor suit, which both girls considered incredibly naff. They couldn't talk, so they waited for the granny to move on, which took some time. When they were gone, Beryl grabbed Carol's hand.

"Hang on a moment. Why *didn't* Tim contact his parents? He promised he would. Maybe he became a ship captain or even an admiral or went off exploring and never came back. Maybe he got married and had a family and decided he never wanted to see them again. Or he moved abroad. Maybe he found his birth parents. Whatever the case, it's possible he doesn't want them to know and prefers being 'dead.' And we would spoil that for him!'

Carol slapped Beryl's thigh hard.

"Clever girl! We need to try and find out what happened to Tim. Maybe he *doesn't* want them to know! Off to the library." There was a faint glimmer of hope, and the girls grabbed it.

As always, Mrs. Norman was happy to see them. She was a tall, thin woman with curly white hair and gold-rimmed spectacles that slid down her nose when she was looking at books. Mrs. Norman seemed stern at first but was lovely and helpful once you got to know her. She had worked there since the library had opened, long before the girls' parents had moved to town.

"Hi, Mrs. Norman." Beryl turned on her charm. "We're doing a school project on the history of the Navy, especially around 1982. Is there anything we can read on that?"

Mrs. Norman smiled.

"Of course, dears. You mean the Falklands War, don't you? I remember that time so well. I was working here, of course. We were all so worried about our brave boys, so far away from home. But amazingly, we won! Great subject for a project. Wait here. I'll get the books." And off she marched.

Beryl and Carol looked at each other with surprise. The Falklands War! They knew nothing about that. It was ancient history. Could that be part of Tim's story?

Mrs. Norman returned with a pile of books, most with pictures of battleships and planes on the cover. "Here you are, dears, plenty to read, you should have an excellent project. And feel free to ask me anything, I know that time so well."

The girls retreated to a corner and read for hours. They hardly knew a thing about this era, but the more they researched it, the more engrossed they became. On the second of April 1982, just two months after Tim's disappearance, England had gone to war with Argentina over the Falkland Islands. The 'Argies' had tried to take back the Islands, but the British Prime Minister, Margaret Thatcher, also known as the 'Iron Lady,' had sent the British Navy 7,500 miles to the south Atlantic Ocean, where a fierce naval battle had taken place. Many soldiers from both sides died at sea and on the Islands. Probably the worst was when *The General Belgrano*, an Argentinian ship, was sunk, and 321 Argentinian sailors lost their lives. By June, the war was over—the Brits had won, and Falkland remained part of the empire.

It was getting late, and the library would be closing in 40 minutes. But there was one more thing they had to find out. They went back to Mrs. Norman.

"Mrs. Norman." Carol's turn to ask. "Was there anyone from around here killed in the Falklands War?"

"Oh, no, dear. I would have known. Two wounded, but not badly, thank God."

Carol fidgeted nervously. "Is there a list of those who died?"

"Oh, yes, I should think so, it would be on microfilm. Let me show you." She took them over to the microfilm machine. The microfilms were strips of film that contained tiny photographs of old records which you viewed on an enlarging machine. Mrs. Norman located the files with the war records and left the girls to it, not before reminding them, "I'm closing in 30 minutes, girls."

Beryl and Carol hardly breathed as they looked at the list of British soldiers killed or Missing in Action during the Falklands War.

There had been 260 casualties overall: sailors, marines, infantry, and airmen. They looked for Marston but could find none.

"Time to go, girls. 5:00 PM. I must close now," Mrs. Norman called.

"Please, Mrs. Norman, just finishing. 5 more minutes max." Beryl used her begging tone.

"Okay, 5 minutes."

One last option. The girls scanned the list for all first names Tim. And finally, there it was: 'Tim Parker, 1964. Missing in Action June, 1982. No next of kin.'

The girls looked at each other, tears in their eyes.

"That was just a few days before the war ended," whispered Carol.

Tim had died at sea, the only place he had ever wanted to live.

CHAPTER 20

Beryl and Carol sat silently, holding hands under the library table and trying to hold back their tears. They thought about Tim and how he might have died, and how they would now definitely have to tell Tim's parents.

Time vanished, until Mrs. Norman called, "Time please, girls, I have to go."

They waited for Mrs. Norman to lock the library and accompanied her home, which was on their way.

"Any questions about the Falklands, dears?" Mrs. Norman loved to chat.

"No, we have loads of stuff, thank you." Beryl searched for a way to say this. "But we were just wondering, wasn't that around the time Tim Marston went missing?"

"Yes, girls. It was." Mrs. Norman didn't hesitate. "I remember it all so well. For two months we were all searching for poor Tim and could not find him, then the war started, and our attention was elsewhere."

"So sad. Did you know him?" They were walking through the park.

"Oh, yes, very well. Tim often came to the library; he was an avid reader. Such a lovely lad. Did you know he was adopted? Mark and Rita, his parents, couldn't have children, so they adopted him when they were quite old. Tim loved them, but maybe they were a bit too old and square for such an energetic boy. He had everything going for him—super smart, a good student, a gentleman, a sportsman, caring and daring, an extraordinary young man. Tim loved camping outdoors and was always off to the forest, which worried his parents.

"He often came to the library to search for his birth parents, but he could never find them. I think they had too common a name to track down, something like Palmer. Such a sad story. The Marstons never recovered after his death. They could not bear to live around here anymore, too many painful memories, so they moved away a couple of years after he disappeared."

They reached Mrs. Norman's house.

Just before they thanked her and bid her goodbye, Beryl asked, "Where are they now, Mrs. Norman? Tim's parents, I mean. Are you in touch with them?"

"Oh, no, dear." Mrs. Norman looked at the girls. "We were in touch for a while, but they both died a few years ago. The heartbreak must have caught up with them eventually."

This changed everything.

When the girls left Mrs. Norman's house, they were overwhelmed by a rollercoaster of emotions. They were trying not to burst into big smiles, but as soon as they were around the corner, they hugged and kissed and high-fived and laughed. Then they thought of the poor Marstons and burst into tears. Then they remembered their secret garden and grinned again. For a few minutes, they hugged and laughed and cried, but finally, they had big grins on their faces. They knew it might be a terrible thing to do, as poor Tim and the Marstons were dead, but they couldn't help it; the relief was enormous. The clearing and their soon-to-be house were safe!

They sat down on the wall outside Beryl's home, swinging their feet. After feeling as heavy as lead, their hearts were light again. Still, there was Tim.

"Poor Tim!" Beryl looked at the ground. "What does Missing in Action mean?"

"Could mean anything," Carol replied slowly. "Maybe he was

shot and fell in the sea, or drowned, or was blown up by a mine or rocket with no remains left. They don't know, because there is no exact date of death."

The girls fell silent. After a while, Beryl brought up the other subject they had avoided so far.

"So, what do you think about the treasure? I've been wondering about it, but I'm not sure it's real. Seems like a fantasy or wishful thinking. He didn't leave much to go by—no map or directions."

Carol didn't answer, but Beryl recognised the faraway look in her friend's eyes. It meant Carol was deep in thought, and Beryl knew her friend would not say anything else until she was ready, so there was no point in interrogating her. But she was pleased Carol was on it—if anyone could work this out, it was Carol.

But when Carol got home, she was in for a nasty surprise. A taxi was waiting outside and by it, her father with a suitcase. Mom and Jerry were there, too, looking down. She knew dad was leaving this week but had forgotten it was today. Carol hugged her dad with all her might, refusing to let him go. Not for the first time that day, she burst into tears. Dad hugged and kissed her, but eventually, he had to leave. The three of them stood on the pavement waving, but there was a huge empty hole left in their hearts. They went inside, but the house seemed dark and empty.

There was nothing to say. Carol went upstairs. On her bed was a note. Carol recognised her father's handwriting. She unfolded it and read silently.

My darling Carol,

I'll miss you every moment of every day. But I'll be back as soon as I possibly can. Remember, I will be home every second weekend, and on school holidays, so I'll be with you in the summer. I can't wait to see you soon.

Maybe we can still find a way to save our house...

I wrote this poem for you!

Every act of strength leads to another act of strength
Every act of weakness leads to another act of weakness
Courage begets courage
Fear breeds fear.

Small acts generate bigger acts
Big acts generate greatness
Facing pain and overcoming difficulties
Enhances freedom and power.

Unexpected solutions are given by heaven
As a token of
Appreciation for honest endeavours
Humility and goodwill.

Life spirals up and down
Snakes and ladders.
At every moment,
Choose your path.

Once decided, don't look back
Move on. Gateways will open.
At all times
The universe is unfolding as it should.

Love always,

Dad.

CHAPTER 21

When the end-of-term maths exam results arrived, Beryl's 'Barely' and Carol's 'Hardly' turned out to be based on an entirely different set of standards. Beryl had flunked with an embarrassing 7%, while Carol shone with 92%, best in class.

"Take that, you lying-Nonco." Beryl repeatedly smacked her friend on the head with her rucksack so that Carol had to duck and run. "There you go telling me you know nothing again!" Carol wished she hadn't gotten such a high score.

"Well, together we have 99%." Carol tried humour. It didn't work.

Beryl threw the bag at her retreating friend, groaning, "Now I'm in the soup."

Beryl *was* in the soup. Her mother's soup.

* * *

"What exactly is the meaning of this, young lady?" Mum waved the exam paper wildly in the air. Beryl was sure Carol's family could hear her mother screaming. They could.

"You do realise that the headmaster told me you will be staying behind a year if your marks continue to drop!" Beryl's stunned expression indicated she had not realised that. Suddenly she was frightened. "No more going out or playing for you. Grounded!"

Beryl's mum continued her full-force rant, slapping the table with the tattered exam paper.

"B… B… but Mum…" Beryl desperately searched for an excuse. But when Beryl's mum was mad, it would have to be a world-class excuse, and Beryl didn't even have a rainy day one.

"Maybe when Carol's family moves to Birmingham, you will have more time to study," Beryl's mum bellowed, all too loudly. As soon as the words had left her lips, she regretted saying them. That was hitting below the belt, and she hadn't meant to do that. But it was too late. Beryl burst into tears, ran off and locked herself in the toilet while her mother prayed that her best friends next door had not heard what she had just said. They had.

It was Beryl's turn to lie awake agonising. Her school reports had always repeated the same idea in a variety of creative ways: 'Beryl is smart, but she does not apply herself.' 'Beryl could do so much better if she only tried a bit harder.' 'Beryl is bright but appears not to put in the required work.' 'If Beryl only spent a fraction of her basketball time studying, she could be a great student.' Etc. Etc. Etc. It was the worst when it came to maths. She had a block about maths. Maybe it was laziness, but she still hated the subject. Anyway, up till now, she *had* been able to get away with doing nothing. Beryl's school motto, which she often proclaimed with a big grin, was: 'Who says nothing's impossible? I've been doing nothing for years!' But the higher level of studies had stealthily crept up on Beryl and was now nipping at her heels. She imagined herself downgraded to the class below, separated from Carol and all her friends, stuck with stupid little kids and looking the fool. She did not like that at all!

* * *

The next morning, Carol knocked on Beryl's door. Beryl was upstairs studying and sulking, not necessarily in that order.

"I am so sorry, Aunt Maria." Carol looked down sheepishly. "It's my fault, for sure. I distracted Beryl because she was trying to help me with all my jobs. I promise you that I will force her to study every day, and I will help her with everything. Please give us a chance." She gave Beryl's mum her Labrador-begging-for-food look. Her deep green eyes were sad and forlorn, her expression authentic (she had practised this look in front of the mirror all morning). The look alone might not have been enough to do the trick, but Maria's deep embarrassment about her neighbours hearing what she had said last night forced her to concede.

"Take your friend and your books, and get the heck out of here now!" Beryl's mother half-scowled and half-smiled. "And if my daughter doesn't have a university degree by this evening, don't come home!"

CHAPTER 22

"Pass the hammer, Nonco." Beryl was trying to speak while holding five nails between her teeth.

"You shut up!" Carol smiled as she passed her the hammer.

This was the kind of chat the girls liked when they were feeling happy, and they had good reason to be happy. Carol flipped Beryl the hammer in a well-practised toss, and Beryl picked another plank from the pile and nailed it diagonally onto the upper corner of the house frame. Her motions were precise and strong, and in no time, the beam was supporting the structure and waiting for more screws to drive it home.

Easter holidays had begun; no more exams, no more school, no more High-Street Gang. They had three weeks to build the house, the weather was perfect, and everything they needed was ready in the clearing. They had got up early, told their mums they were off to revise schoolwork and play, walked through the park for their alibi, and then sneaked into the forest. Pushing the Kon-Taki upriver seemed like too much hard work on a gorgeous day like this.

It was now near noon, and the frame was beginning to take shape. The girls stuck posts into six holes they had dug, then squashed stones and earth around each one to make them firm. They attached the posts with crossbars at the middle and top. They were singing as they worked, The Beatles, Elvis, 'Summertime,' and other golden oldies which Beryl's dad had introduced them to in his 'Rock n' Roll Lessons.'

When the frame was finished, Carol gave the structure a shake, and it barely moved—it was stable! Once they covered the sides with plywood, it would be… well, as strong as houses! It looked fantastic, and for the first time, they could believe that their dream could come true—they would have their own home.

The next step was the walls. The girls used the eight pieces of plywood they had 'rescued' from an abandoned building site. They took turns, one of them holding the board in place and the other using Beryl's dad's battery-powered screwdriver to screw it onto the frame. It would have taken hours if they'd had to screw or drill by hand, but the electric tools did it in a few seconds. In a little over an hour, plywood walls were covering the whole frame.

Beryl and Carol were ecstatic. They danced around the house, then in and out through the door frame, singing 'Our house, is a very, very, very, nice house.' The house felt pleasant and welcoming inside, and just the right size. They dragged the tarpaulin inside and spread it on the ground, covering it with mats and rugs. They brought in their table and the box seat and placed them near the future kitchen. Carol put a vase with flowers on the table. They had a home!

Of course, there was still a lot of work to be done. They would have to fix the windows and door, install some shelves, waterproof the bottom of the walls, build the porch, and lots more. But it had been a tremendous start, and they had achieved much more than they had expected on the first day. But even as they danced around the house, sat by the kitchen table, and lay on the mattress, they both knew they were ignoring the biggest issue.

"One problem left." Beryl looked up at the sky.

"I know," Carol groaned. She had been thinking the same thing. "No wood for a roof."

"We've looked all over," said Beryl. "Nowhere else I can think of."

The girls had explored the entire village in their search for building materials. They had burrowed in every skip, visited every building site, and combed the rubbish dump. Most of the stuff they found was free, and the only wood they had bought were the six posts for the frame. But nowhere had they been able to find materials for the roof.

"Lucky there's no rain forecast for tomorrow." Beryl tried to lighten the atmosphere.

"But there is major rain forecast for next week." Carol darkened the atmosphere back.

The girls walked home silently, not saying a word. By now, they did not need to look at tree markings, they knew every root and bush on the way. They were flooded with mixed feelings—on the one hand, the joy that they had achieved so much in one day and had a house standing, and on the other, the problem of no roof and the looming storm.

Before they parted, Beryl turned to her friend but looked at the ground as she spoke. She knew that what she was going to say would not be well received.

"Carol. A house without a roof is not a house. Rain is coming. You know as well as I do that if the wood gets wet and the floor becomes a mud bath, our house will be ruined. We have no choice. We need to buy the wood. How much money have you saved?"

That's when the argument began.

CHAPTER 23

Carol had been doing everything she could to make money and save every penny. As the weeks passed, more jobs had been rolling in. Most of the jobs were downright miserable. She was teaching maths to problematic kids three times a week. She mowed lawns, washed cars, walked dogs, and worst of all, cleaned toilets at the Pizza shop. She abstained from buying any essentials, such as ice cream (except once), chocolate, books, trinkets, or going to the cinema. Every night she counted her savings, calculating how much more she needed before she could rescue her home and stop her father from leaving.

The way Carol saw it, she was working to save her life and the lives of all those around her, and there could be no compromise. Making the money she needed became an obsession, and though she realised she was a long way off, that made her even more determined. And now Beryl, who had not worked half as much as her, was asking her to give up her savings! She found it difficult to believe.

"What?!" Carol went ballistic. "No way are you getting your grubby fingers on my hard-earned cash!"

"But... Carol, b... but please be reasonable," Beryl stuttered. She had been expecting a strong reaction, but this was far worse than she had imagined. Beryl underestimated how hard Carol had worked and how important it was to her.

"But my butt! No one is getting my money." And with that, Carol turned around, stomped into her house, and slammed the front door.

* * *

For the next three days, the girls didn't see or talk to each other. It was not often they argued, but it happened occasionally. Beryl had a hot temper but would cool down quickly, while Carol tended to go silent and brood for quite a while. She sat in her room, sulking for two days, then went swimming at the town pool. Being underwater soothed her anger and drowned out all the chatter in her mind. While she swam, she concentrated on perfecting her technique, working out problems, or revising lessons. Anyway, she wasn't into team sports. Carol liked to measure her progress against herself and not others.

Beryl *was* into team sports and decided she might as well practise her basketball. After all, she was the team captain. Beryl was upset about what had happened with Carol but was not one to sit around moping.

When she arrived at the court early the next morning, she found Jerry, Carol's brother, practising basketball on his own. Jerry was 17. He had always been her best friend's older brother, distant and aloof, so they never spoke much, but when it came to sports, Jerry became fun and friendly. They ended up playing for hours every day and never said a word about Carol. Jerry had lots to teach, and that was precisely what Beryl loved—improving her game. They practised dribbling and passing and long shots and near shots and trick shots. Most importantly, Jerry taught Beryl cuts.

Cuts were a way of running rings around the opposition. You pretended to move or throw the ball in one direction, then suddenly swerved in the other direction, leaving the opponent wrong-footed and wondering where you had vanished. There were Backdoor-Cuts, V-Cuts, and L-Cuts. Beryl had never imagined such smart moves existed. Playing basketball all day was heaven. Beryl didn't think much about Carol while she was on the court, but when she came home in the evening, she saw the lonely light in Carol's window and felt sorry she had upset her friend. She was eager to get on with building the house, though without a roof, it seemed like a dead end.

* * *

Beryl lay in bed thinking of what had happened and could find no way out, so when her mother came to say goodnight, she spoke to her about the quarrel, leaving out the details.

Mum thought for a while and said, "Friendships need good fights occasionally, just as every child needs a good fever once in a while. Fevers burn out infections, bacteria, viruses, and toxins, so they are an essential part of a healthy life. Fights are similar; they are fires that clean out all the little tensions that build up in a relationship, so they bring true friends closer together. That's why Dad and I are often closer after a good quarrel. After a fight, it becomes easier to see the other person's point of view, say sorry, and move on. My motto on this is, 'Fight, fever, forgive, forget, freedom.'"

By the time Mum had finished explaining, a very tired Beryl was fast asleep. But the lesson had sunk in.

And so, after three days of not talking, Beryl stood outside Carol's house and threw pebbles at her window. Carol refused to answer, though she knew very well it was Beryl. But after the eighth pebble, Carol couldn't stand it any longer. She went to the window and looked down, and there was Beryl holding up a huge sign which read:

'I'M SORRY!!!'

Carol pulled a face, left the window, and was gone. Beryl stood there not knowing what to do, her heart pounding and a tear running down her cheek. She waited for a while, but Carol did not return. Beryl was distressed. What had she done?! She knew how important saving her parents' house was to Carol and how hard she had worked for every penny. She should never have asked for that money. Had she lost her best friend?

Just as Beryl was about to give up and go home, Carol reappeared at the window with a sign which read:

'92 POUNDS AND 51 PENNIES.'

Beryl smiled, wiping her eyes. It was going to be okay.

CHAPTER 24

When the girls met the next morning, they did not mention the argument. They just did the short handshake and moved on. Carol said nothing of Beryl's time with Jerry, although she had heard her brother raving about what a talented player Beryl was.

Instead, she pointed to town and grunted in her cavewoman voice, "Rain coming, build roof."

"Aye, aye, Captain." Beryl was being extra nice.

The new sheets of plywood and tar paper that the girls bought at the DIY store would be delivered to Mrs. E's house later that morning. They correctly assumed that their parents would think the new owners were doing renovations. Seeing the girls had very little spare change left, they decided it would be best to put the money to good use, so they went to the ice cream shop. It had been too long.

It was while they were standing outside the corner shop savouring their ice cream that they noticed the local paper's headline, in large red letters:

'*Princess Diana to open new children's hospice and become patron.*' And under that, in black type, '*Mark the date in your diaries! Wednesday, October the 8ᵗʰ.*' There was a picture of the Princess, one they had seen many time times before.

The girls were huge fans of Diana.

"Wow."

"Wow."

"Wow, wow, wow!"

"I can't wait to see the Princess live! The first royal visit here ever. Unbelievable." Carol finished her ice cream in one bite, which was usually considered a huge mistake. "If the Princess becomes patron of the new hospice, it could bring lots of jobs to town. And jobs make work for accountants!"

"You know they call her the Queen of Hearts." Beryl licked the last bits of ice cream off her fingers. "Well, I think she should be called the Queen of Diamonds. You know, Di for Diamonds, and she always wears a diamond tiara."

"The Queen of Diamonds it is." Carol was impressed.

By the time they got home, the small truck with the wood and tar paper was standing outside Mrs. E's house.

"Finally, a sign of life." Beryl's dad looked through the window. "Our new neighbours have only visited once since they bought the place. Must be starting by fixing the shed. Smart move."

"Can we go and see, Dad?" Beryl asked innocently.

"Sure, but don't get in the way."

The two girls showed the workmen where to store the wood behind Mrs. E's garden shed.

Once the truck left, Beryl and Carol loaded the plywood sheets onto the Kon Taki. They pushed the raft upriver, which was a struggle, but one hour later, they sat under the oak, exhausted from the journey, wet and puffing.

"Weatherman says it's rain in two days." Beryl looked at the gathering clouds. "But I'm honestly too whacked to do any more work today."

Carol could hardly find the energy to nod, so she groaned instead.

The girls sat catching their breath for a while longer, and then Beryl said softly, "Thanks for buying the wood, Dame Peril. I really appreciate it."

Carol looked at her friend. "I thought long and hard about it. I earned nearly 100 pounds in 6 weeks. How many years would it take me to earn 20,000?"

"Around 25 years, if you didn't eat any ice cream," Beryl replied immediately.

Carol was surprised at how quickly her friend had calculated it. She nodded.

"Yep, 25 years. At that rate, I would be 37 years old when I get all the money. And I'm not abstaining from ice cream for that long! There's no point in carrying on. I have to find another way. But meanwhile, better that we have one house than no house. If we finish this house and my family moves, I can run away from home, and we can live here together."

Beryl was quiet for a while. She had not seen it this way before, but it was suddenly crystal clear.

She stood up and declared, "My energy is back. Let's build a roof."

CHAPTER 25

It was on the last day of the Easter holidays when the girls considered the house ready. The weather had been patchy, so they worked extra hard between bouts of rain, but they had loved every minute of it. The pleasure of building their own house was the best feeling they had ever known, and they almost regretted that the house was finished.

New sheets of plywood covered the roof and porch, and on top of these were layers of waterproof tar paper. The doors and windows were in place, which was much harder to do than they had expected and had taken them two days. They had put up shelves in the kitchen and bedroom area and arranged all their gear on them—pots and pans, cutlery, games, books, and clothes. The mattress was covered with a sheet and a bedspread, and pictures were hanging on the walls.

There was plenty more that needed finishing, painting the wood, building a cupboard in the kitchen, and perhaps bringing an armchair or two for relaxing and reading. But it was a home they could live in, and the rest of the work could be done slowly over the long summer holidays.

The girls could hardly believe they had built such a perfect house themselves and felt sorry they could not show it to their parents. Of course, if their parents ever found out, they would be grounded for life. Anyway, not having parents to boss them around was a huge bonus!

"Yayyy!" Beryl jumped up and down, clapping her hands. "We did it! We actually built a house!"

"Yes, and one day we will actually live here!"

They hugged and did a little dance followed by the extended version of their secret handshake.

"We need a code name for our house." Beryl had obviously thought about this. "I have an idea—Meukki. You say it like Murky, but without the R. It means 'a summer cottage' in Finnish, usually a cute log cabin by the water. I stayed at my aunt's Meukki last summer. So, this can be *our* Meukki."

Carol was reluctant, but she decided to hide it. "Okay. You're right, we need a secret name. No one will understand what we mean if we say, 'Let's go to the Meukki.' Except maybe your mum."

Beryl grinned. She was always happy to have something Finnish involved.

Tomorrow was the first day back to school; Beryl and Carol would have to face over-enthusiastic teachers, pushy parents, swimming, basketball, final projects, and end-of-year shows. And nasty bullies.

But they had a house.

And Carol had a plan.

CHAPTER 26

"Don't you think you've spent enough time picnicking and playing over the holidays, young lady?" Beryl's mum said when she caught her trying to sneak out on Saturday morning. "You've got a hard last term ahead of you, and you're failing maths. Your history isn't doing well either. I think a quiet weekend studying and helping at home would do you the world of good!"

"But Mum…" Beryl pleaded. "That's exactly what I'm planning! Carol and I have a study date in the park. History and maths. Not saying we won't play a bit, Mum, but study we will."

Mum gave her a sceptical look.

"And what about some help at home? You're still part of this family, you know."

"Sure, Mum. Washing up is on me tonight, I promise. Got to run now, Mum. Carol is waiting and very eager to study." Beryl made a hasty getaway before Mum could think of anything else.

* * *

The clearing was as pretty as they had ever seen it. New flowers were blooming, colourful anemones and violets. And there, under the oak, stood their little house, green with red trimmings, looking as if it had lived there forever. And now it could remain there forever—there was no need to destroy it! It was their secret home, their Meukki, and they loved it.

"Time for the ceremony." Beryl got her bag. The girls walked over to the fallen tree near the willow, which they often used as a riverside bench. Beryl took out the wooden sign she had prepared at home. She had cut off the end of a log, sanded it down until it was smooth, then scorched letters on it using the sun's rays shining through a magnifying glass. Then she varnished the wood and drilled two holes in the sides. The plaque looked professionally done. She took two screws and fastened it to the log.

Carol fetched the tobacco tin with Tim's note wrapped in a new plastic bag, together with the rose cutting she had bought from home. It was a species called *Rosa Carolina*. Her mother had planted it for Carol when she was born. The friends buried the box and planted the rose stem next to the plaque. Then they placed a flat slab of rock over where the tin was buried.

The shrine was ready.

They stood solemnly for a moment, then Beryl read the words she had burnt onto the log:

"Tim Parker Marston. 1964. Lost at sea during the Falklands War, June, 1982. R.I.P."

They sat on the log near Tim. They were the only ones who knew how he had died, and now they had honoured him in the place he loved. Beryl laid another flower on the flat stone, and Carol put a small rock on it, a custom she had learnt from her Jewish grandmother.

"I wish we could have met Tim and shared the clearing with him," Carol said sadly. "I'm sure we would have got on well—he had spirit and brains and a sense of adventure, and he followed his truth."

A gift for you

It's all the rage at AHE! Book contest: how many times is Jeremy's name mentioned & can you identify keynotes of Platina? Includes names of well know homeopaths. What a great way to embed homeopathy in young minds! From Rooksie David

Beryl wished that too. Tim was special.

"Well, I guess that's that," said Beryl a little despondently. Beryl liked action. Finishing the house and the ceremony had left an empty space in their lives—nothing more to do.

"Er… actually no, that is not that," replied Carol.

"What are you talking about?" Beryl was puzzled.

"Well, Nonco, what about the treasure?"

"I thought that was a tall story or a dead end, we have no clues and nothing at all to go by. You said nothing all this time, so I thought you gave up and forgot about it." Beryl sat up straight, excited now. "You mean you found something?"

Carol yawned and said nothing. She knew how to tease Beryl's impatient nature.

"Come on, tell me! Did you find anything?" Beryl urged.

"Mmmm, maybe later. I'm a bit tired." Carol was enjoying stretching this out.

"You better tell me right now, or you're in the river. All this time, and you said nothing!" Beryl tried to slap her friend on the head.

Carol was expecting it, so she ducked and laughed.

"Okay, you shut up and listen."

CHAPTER 27

"First of all, here is what the note says." Carol pulled a note out of her unopened history book. She showed it to Beryl. It was a handwritten copy of Tim's letter, the part about the treasure.

"I've read this note a hundred times. I know it off by heart," said Carol, which was designed to make Beryl even more impressed, and it worked. "There's a lot to learn from it."

"Like what? That there is a treasure somewhere?"

"Much more." Carol was in Sherlock Holmes mode. "We know that the treasure is near a waterfall. But it seems that it is a place that was too small for Tim to enter, a cave or hole perhaps. And we can assume that he found out about it in books, because there was no internet at the time."

"Clever you!" Beryl complimented. "But there are no falls around here."

"Wrong, again, Nonco," said Carol. "We just have to look further. I've checked maps of the area, and there are three waterfalls within walking distance, on another river which connects to ours upstream. The closest fall is five miles away, the furthest about twelve. It could be at any one of them. We have to get to these falls and explore them, looking for somewhere with a small hole or burrow to crawl into."

"Right…" Beryl was all ears.

"Then we have to find out what treasure it could be. When I

realised Tim must have found the information in a book, I visited Mrs. Norman and asked her if she still had the list of books Tim borrowed. Of course, with Mrs. Norman being Mrs. Norman, she still had the list, which was quite long. I looked through it, and there it was: *The Lost and Stolen Treasures of Britain for Young Readers*. Bingo."

Beryl was full of admiration for Carol's thoroughness. She knew this was how she was, and she loved her all the more for it.

"I've read the book," Carol continued, "but unfortunately, Tim didn't mark the page, so I couldn't find it from there. There are loads of missing and stolen treasures. I made a list." Carol extracted another sheet of paper from her history book. "King John's stolen jewels in the 13th century. Lots of shipwrecks, like the £120 million haul of gold which went down with the 'Royal Charter' when it sank during a hurricane in the 1850s. Queen Victoria's parliamentary mace, stolen in 1891. Loads of people find ancient Roman or Anglo-Saxon coins. But mostly it's stolen art.

"I couldn't find anything that mentions our county, so it's difficult to tell what it was. But I found some other books that Tim was reading, *Forests and Natural Attractions of Wales and Western England* and *Smugglers of the Irish Sea*. He also studied maps of the area, guidebooks, and nature books. I still have to read those. It's obvious Tim was onto something. So, we have quite a bit to go on."

Carol paused for effect, then carried on.

"We know the treasure is by the falls, so we need to find a way to get there, and that will take more than one day, but I have that all worked out."

"I'm sure you do!" Beryl gushed, full of excitement. "Come on, tell me."

"Well," Carol continued, "to walk to all three falls and explore them, I estimate we need four or five days, depending on how lucky we are, and which falls we are talking about. That means summer holidays, and it means staying here at our house for a few days, which of course our parents won't allow."

"No way they will." Beryl looked downcast.

"Except that I found the 'Green River Campsite' on the other side of the river, about a mile downstream, just below where the waterfall river meets with ours. The campsite was marked in one of Tim's guidebooks. I enquired, and children over 12 years old can camp there alone because they have a guard on site. We just need our parents' permission. No one has to know if we sneak back to our Meukki after we pitch our tent. We'll sleep here, then slip back in the mornings to show our faces, then go for 'hikes' and come back in the evening. That way we get to live in our Meukki! And all we need is to build a simple little bridge, just two logs across the narrow point down the river."

"But our parents will never…"

"Got that sorted, Nonco. First of all, the camp leaders are a Mr. and Mrs. Phillips. Yes, exactly, the Mrs. Phillips who was our Girl Guide District Leader. Remember her from camp? What could be safer! She offers kids-only camps and activities there. And our mums adore her. That'll make a huge difference. Next is a two-pronged attack. Emotional blackmail with my mother. That's already done, they had no choice because they are feeling so guilty about us moving to Birmingham. I cried and wailed a lot, and they finally agreed. Now we just have to use emotional bribery with your mum. And that, my dearest best friend in the world, means you'll be getting over 90% in maths!"

"But, Carol, I have a block about maths. I just don't get it."

"I think you *do* have a block, but not about maths. It's a block about work, you Nonco." Carol smiled. "I think you're so smart that until now you could get away with zero studies, so you missed the basics, and now you think you can't do maths. All that changes right now. I happen to know you *are* very good at it. So starting tomorrow, we're going to spend two hours a day working on your maths. *Seriously*, no messing about. Because at the moment that treasure is our only chance of me keeping my home next door to you, where I belong. And it beats cleaning toilets at the Pizza place. I already spoke to my mum about it. We can sit in her office and she'll help, she's ace at maths."

Beryl's mouth opened, closed, then opened again, making her look a bit like a goldfish.

Carol folded her notes. "You see, it's all worked out, Nonco."

Beryl was too excited to even say, "You shut up."

CHAPTER 28

Everything was ready. Carol laid the camping equipment she got for her birthday on Beryl's lawn. A brand-new blue tent for two that could withstand winds of up to 90 miles an hour ('Not likely around here,' said Beryl). It had a front porch, hooks to hang stuff from, pockets to stuff things in, and a built-in lamp. The girls did a practice pitch in the garden and found it easy to put up, comfortable, and roomy. They hoped to be sleeping at their Meukki and not the tent, but they would have to visit during the daytime.

Their mums had organised a large box of food full of vegetables, fruit, rice, pasta, bread, spreads, and biscuits. There were plastic tupperware boxes with readymade stews and curries, and a gorgeous carrot cake from Beryl's mum with an icing picture of a tent and a tree on it. Plus a basket full of fruit and juice.

"It's enough for an army, Mum!" Beryl could not believe the amount of food they had.

"I won't have my girls starving," Mum insisted.

"No chance of that, Mum." Beryl pointed at the huge boxes.

"I still can't believe you got 93% in maths," said Beryl's mother for the nineteenth time. "I'd never have agreed to that deal with Carol if I'd thought you would. I was sure you'd flunk it! I think you deliberately tricked me by playing lazy all these years."

"That girl is a slave driver, Mum." Beryl flashed a wide grin and pointed at Carol. "But also, the best maths teacher I ever had. Never underestimate the Peril! And Aunt Naomi really helped a lot. Like mother, like daughter."

"They did work hard." Naomi nodded and looked at her daughter proudly, she knew how badly Carol wanted to help her friend. "Even Mr. Duffy was flabbergasted."

Carol blushed.

"Are you sure it's safe?" Carol's dad asked for the umpteenth time.

"Safe as houses, Pops." Carol gave Dad her well-practised responsible look. "Mrs. Phillips, our old Girl Guides leader, is there and she knows us really well. She's a pro at anything outdoorsy. They have loads of kids camps and activities. They have a fence and a guard, and they welcome kids over 12 camping on their own. We've got to develop those outdoor skills, you know!"

"Indeed, indeed." Carol's dad gave Beryl's dad an 'Are-you-really-sure-it's-safe?' look.

"No worries, Isaac," Carl assured him. "I know the campsite well, used to camp there myself as a lad—very safe. As long as they stay in or nearby the site, they will be fine. And Mrs. Phillips... no one better to look after them!"

"Just remember to phone three times every day." Carol's mum looked anxious. "Or I'll die of worry." That was the Jewish way of saying 'please keep in touch.'

"We will, Mum, promise." Carol did a Brownies promise sign.

They packed all the stuff into Beryl's dad's car, kissed their mums goodbye sixteen times, and hugged Sam and a reluctant Jerry. Off they went, singing 'We're all going on a summer holiday.' Just under an hour later, Carl dropped them at the Green River Camp Site and helped to unload their equipment.

Mrs. Phillips greeted them at the entrance. It was good to see her again. The girls had been Brownies under her for two years, and when she became District Leader, they often saw her at camp. She was red haired, tall, and confident, not a big talker but always kind. She wore her Girl Guides uniform, decorated with loads of badges, pins, and medals. Mrs. Phillips had obviously been around.

She shook their hands warmly.

"Welcome to Green Camp!" she beamed. "Good to see you here, Carol and Beryl. So pleased to see you two are carrying on the Brownie tradition and honing those outdoor skills." Then she turned to Beryl's dad and said, "Good to see you, too, Carl. You can be sure the girls will be safe with us. Mr. Phillips and I are always around, George the guard is on duty, and we have a very secure fence. We run lots of kids camps here. In fact, a group will be coming towards the end of the week, and the girls can join in with their activities. So, sleep soundly and send my best regards to Maria and to Carol's parents. Now, girls, let's go and meet Mr. Phillips. He runs the camp day to day, and I'm busy getting ready for our next Brownies group. But I will be checking in on you."

They waved goodbye to Beryl's dad, who seemed much happier, and followed Mrs. Phillips to the office. She introduced her husband and went off to do some errands.

Mr. Phillips, the camp manager, was sitting at his desk, but he rose to greet them. He was a strong-looking man with sandy hair, a rugged face, and huge hands. He was wearing a khaki shirt, short pants, and walking boots—obviously the outdoor type. Beryl, who possessed the magical gift of making anyone feel special, launched a charm campaign. In no time, Mr. Phillips was relating his life story, and there was no stopping him. He told the girls about his Boy Scout days in this area, how he studied geography at Manchester University, how he became a nature guide and eventually camp manager.

"Used to camp in this site as a young lad." Mr. Phillips was in full swing. "That's why I feel it is so important to let young people like you camp here alone, even if you are only 12." He had not asked for their exact ages. Beryl conveniently ignored the fact that she still had a month until her 12th birthday. "You need to learn outdoor skills and connect to nature. But we make sure it's safe. This brochure will let you know about the available outdoor activities." He handed them a brochure each. "Anyway, girls, no one alive knows the falls area as well as I do. So if you aim to do some hiking, I can tell you some interesting places to visit.'

"Really! That's amazing." Beryl shifted her chat mode up a gear. "Because the reason we chose this campsite is that we are doing our summer school project on waterfalls and caves in the area. It would be really helpful if you could tell us something about them."

"Well, you have come to the right address, ladies." Mr. Phillips was enthusiastic about someone sharing his passion. "I have some work to do right now, but pop in this evening and I'll tell you all you need to know and give you some books."

Beryl and Carol were excited. This was excellent news. They left the office and went off to explore the campsite. The lawn was large and well-kept, surrounded by trees and situated next to the river. In the centre was a communal eating area with picnic tables and place for a bonfire, and behind the main office was a shower block and a large fridge where they could store food. There were only a few tents because it was early in the holiday, which suited the girls just fine.

They walked around the site and found a perfect spot near the river, hidden from the rest of the camp by a cluster of birch trees. They pitched their tent with the porch facing the fence and the river, which was not unusual, people liked to sit in front of their tents and watch the water. Everything was working out fine.

The girls hi-fived—this was a dream come true, they were free. Five whole days with no school or parents, in their lovely Meukki, and with a treasure hunt to boot. They were itching to get to their house. Beryl examined the fence. It was tall with nasty looking barbed wire curled on top, but the chicken mesh itself was not too thick.

"Once we pitch the tent, we can cut a flap, so we can open and close it like a door, and then escape to the Meukki."

"Are you sure?" Carol suddenly seemed uncertain, although it was her plan. "They might find out we're gone, and it could be dangerous at night."

Beryl was adamant.

"Danger is our middle name, Nonco. It's only a mile up the river to the bridge."

The bridge was two logs they had laid across the narrowest point in the river, making sure the ends were well secured with stones. They had crawled over it on their hands and knees, and it wasn't difficult. After crossing the bridge, it would be a short walk to their clearing. Everything was going according to plan. Tonight, for the first time, they would be sleeping in their own little house.

Once the tent was up, they prepared lunch and had a picnic next to the tent, avoiding the other campers, as they didn't want people getting friendly and nosing around. They packed small bags ready for their nighttime trip to the Meukki and read for a while. Beryl got out the wire cutters she had 'borrowed' from her dad, and while Carol stood guard to make sure no one was coming, Beryl cut a flap in the wire fence. She tried opening it and going through to the other side, then she closed it so that no one could see the cut.

They walked over to the phone booth to call their mums,

assuring them that everything was okay, emphasising again and again how safe they felt. But it seemed that once they were out of sight, their mums were enjoying the peace and were less worried. Good, fewer phone calls needed. Next, they went to visit the guard in his little hut by the front gate, armed with a slice of carrot cake.

George was a chubby man with bushy white eyebrows and an old blue baseball cap who didn't look as if he could guard a chicken coop. But he seemed happy for the opportunity to talk to someone.

"Best cake I had in ages!" George spluttered crumbs everywhere.

"Glad you like it! We'll bring some more tomorrow." Beryl smiled.

"What time do you close for the night?" Carol pointed at the large iron gate.

"Oh, around 8:00 PM when it starts getting dark." George wiped more scraps of cake from his blue shirt. "Don't worry girls, you'll be safe as houses."

The girls smiled. They planned to be safe in *their* house.

"Oh, that's very comforting." Beryl acted the helpless girl. "We feel safe with you around, George."

"Of course you do, and Mrs. Phillips or me will be coming round to check on you every few hours."

That changed everything.

CHAPTER 29

The girls walked away from George's hut feeling miserable. They had not foreseen Mrs. Phillips or George checking their tent at night. This put their whole scheme in jeopardy.

"What can we do? This will ruin our plan of sleeping at our house." Beryl was upset.

Carol was also disappointed, but secretly a little relieved.

"I think we have to stay here tonight. It's only the first night, let's see how well Mrs. Phillips or George check us and even let them know we are in the tent and okay, so they can relax and maybe stop checking."

"But I really, really, want to sleep at our house tonight. What's the point of a house if you can't sleep in it?"

"We will, I want to sleep there, too. I promise I'll find a way. But the main goal is to find the treasure, and maybe being here will help us focus on that. How about we talk to Mr. Phillips?"

Beryl was disappointed but reluctantly agreed, so they walked over to the office and knocked on the door.

"Oh, hi, ladies." Mr. Phillips was tidying up his desk. "Nearly finished, come on in and have a seat. Can I get you something to drink? Water? Tea?"

They took some water and waited while Mr. Phillips filed his papers away. He was clearly efficient and conscientious about his work. His office was tidy and well organised, each file neatly marked with a colored tab. Carol made a mental note to be just like that. Beryl didn't.

"Well, now." Mr. Phillips sat down and folded his big fingers in front of him. "If you want to do a project on the falls and caves, you have come to the right address!" He beamed with pride. "Not only are we the closest campsite to the waterfalls, but I have spent most of my life exploring and studying this area. It's my passion, as well as my profession."

The girls were eager to hear more.

"Please tell us whatever you can, Mr. Phillips." Carol took out her notebook and pen.

"As you probably know, there are three falls," Mr. Phillips explained. "The first is about five miles away, two hours walk along the river. It's a nice spot but a bit too touristy for my taste. I often swam there as a boy, and no one was ever around, but now it's a family picnic area. That's the way the world goes, I guess.

"The second falls are upriver, about nine miles away. They are much taller, about 12 feet, and very beautiful. They're just on the edge of the forest. But the third falls are the largest and most spectacular, about 25 feet high. Because they are deep in the woods, not many people ever go there, too far for a day's walk. But you can easily get there and back in a half a day on our mountain bikes. You can pick them up from George tomorrow."

"That sounds wonderful," said Carol, frantically taking notes. "Where would we find the caves, Mr. Phillips? Are they large or small? Would we be able to go inside?"

"Well," Mr. Phillips explained, "there are about six or seven of them in the cliff around the large falls. One big one was where stone age people lived, and some say smugglers used to hide in. The others are just burrows, or tunnels in the cliff face, too small for a grown man to enter. And there is one small tunnel that hardly anyone knows about because it's hidden right behind the falls. That was my secret, but I could never get inside because it was too small for me to crawl into, even as a teenager."

Carol looked up from her notebook, now all ears. Out of the corner of her eye, she saw Beryl stiffen in her chair. The girls were bristling with excitement, but they managed to remain calm on the outside.

Carol thought about asking if he thought they could fit in the smaller caves, but she decided against it. It might arouse Mr. Phillips's suspicions. Instead, she said,

"Are there any caves by the second fall?"

"No, they're all around the big falls. I'll give you a book on the Geology and History of the area." Mr. Phillips pulled out a well-worn paperback from his bookshelf and handed it to Carol. "That should provide you with enough theoretical material to write about. But, of course, there's nothing like visiting the place yourself. You can be there in a two to three hour bike ride. There's still a path, though it's a bit overgrown. People don't go there much since Tim Marston vanished in these woods, even though everyone knows that wasn't the part of the forest he was in, which is why this area is perfectly safe. Have you heard about Tim Marston, girls?"

The girls nodded. They had heard from Tim directly, but they weren't going to admit that.

"Let me tell you something not many people know." Mr. Phillips suddenly looked sad. "Tim was my best friend. We were the same age—I met him at the Boy Scouts. We hiked and camped around here, and often biked to the falls together. They were Tim's special place, and he knew everything there was to know about them. That's why I told you that I know the area better than anyone alive, but not as well as Tim did, bless his soul. He spent every day of his holidays hiking all over this forest, and during school he would read all he could about the area. He was a super nice and super clever guy. A big tragedy for me, him vanishing like that. I miss him to this very day."

You could have knocked Carol and Beryl over with a feather.

CHAPTER 30

When the girls left Mr. Phillips's office, they were bubbling with excitement. As soon as they were out of sight, they gave each other double high fives. They could hardly contain themselves.

"Bingo!" said Carol.

"Jackpot!" said Beryl.

"Hole in one!" said Carol.

"Bullseye!" said Beryl.

"Goal!" said Carol.

They continued with various declarations of glee while dancing a little jig.

"We're on the right track," said Beryl, "thanks to your good detective work, Dame Peril."

"I guess I was lucky," Carol laughed. They both knew luck had nothing to do with it.

"Now we know who Tim's friend was! And we know the third falls must be the place where the treasure is hidden," said Beryl. "It *was* a smuggler's den!"

"And we know that there is a hidden cave behind the falls," Carol finished the train of thought.

The girls went back to their tent, feeling very pleased with themselves. After dinner, they sat by the tent's front porch looking at the river, eating cake, and enjoying no-parent peace.

"I wonder if the treasure is hidden in the cave. It can't be too big if it is." Beryl poured some more hot chocolate.

"Well, I hope it's a real treasure and not fake and worthless. I think it might be a scrolled-up painting, and we'll sell it to get the money to save my house. But the main question is, can we fit inside the cave? Mr. Phillips or Tim couldn't. More likely you than me."

Beryl shuddered. She was petrified of closed narrow spaces. But she was the slimmer of the two, so it was obviously going to be her.

"I know," said Carol sympathetically. "I promise I'll go in if I can fit. Meanwhile, no more cake for you! We need you Simon." She made a grab for Beryl's carrot cake.

"You will fit in that cave; I can't do it!" Beryl slapped Carol's hand away.

The girls were silent for a while, thinking of all the options and possibilities.

Beryl stood up and yawned. "Let's get an early night, so we can leave first thing in the morning."

By 8:30 the following morning, the girls were heading for the falls on mountain bikes. They cycled alongside the river until they came to the place where their river was joined by another river. Then they cycled upstream on the narrow path which ran alongside the riverbank.

Riding the bikes felt terrific. The bicycles were in good shape, the path was well-marked, and the weather was pleasant. There was not a person in sight. The girls relished navigating the curves and bumps, feeling the wind in their hair, and smelling the delicate scents of flowers rising from the fields to their right. On their left, the river flowed. Once in a while, they saw a colourful bird dipping its wings in the water or a small animal scuttling the bank. This is what freedom felt like!

After half an hour of cycling, the girls saw a sign pointing to the first waterfall. They followed a short trail off the main path and before long they were there. The waterfall was small, about 4 or 5 feet high, with a pond at the bottom where you could swim. Carol suddenly remembered picnicking there with her family when she was 4 or 5 years old. It brought back a flood of memories; splashing in the pool with Mum and playing hide and seek with Jerry and Dad. She felt sad but was not sure why.

The area was pleasant but too touristy. There were picnic tables, a BBQ corner, and a sign describing the geology and local wildlife, so it was a place where people came to spend the day. But it was early on a weekday, so no one was there yet.

"Quick swim?" If Carol saw water, she had to get in it.

"No way, Nonco. We have a long bike ride ahead. You can swim in the last falls." Beryl got back on her bike.

By ten in the morning, they arrived at the second falls. Just as Mr. Phillips had said, these were much prettier—higher and broader, splashing down onto water-smoothed rocks and gathering in a pool surrounded by water flowers. There was a nice shady area around the pond, with rocks to sit on and grass to lie on.

"Tempting," said Carol, wishing she could jump in the pond. "Maybe we should come back tomorrow or the next day."

Beryl agreed, but they had to push on. There was a small sign pointing to the third falls. It directed them to a path which entered the forest. The trail was partly overgrown, and it seemed as though very few people walked or biked here. The ride was bumpy, and occasionally they would hit a root or have to duck to miss a branch. This was real mountain-biking, and once the girls learnt to handle the obstacles, it was great fun.

Half an hour later they could hear the roar of falling water, and ten minutes after that they were at the large falls.

If there was any treasure to be found, it would be here.

CHAPTER 31

The falls were awe-inspiring, though they were not as pretty as the second falls. They were set against a massive cliff, and their height dwarfed the first two falls. There was a large cave opening to the left, and a few smaller holes dotted the cliff face. The water cascaded forcefully down the cliff, gathered in a small pond, and immediately continued into the river. The bank was overgrown with plants, roots, and trees, which would make walking alongside the river difficult. The environment wasn't convenient for picnics—no grass and nowhere to sit, the water was too noisy, and it was too far from the main path. The girls supposed that was why people didn't visit often.

The friends stood watching the thundering water, enjoying the fine mist on their faces. After a while, Beryl walked towards the cave, trying to avoid the worst of the spray, and Carol followed. They clambered over a few rocks to the cave's entrance, which was about three metres wide. The opening was littered with rocks and old beer cans. The girls hesitated before going in. Carol shouted, 'Hello?' into the mouth of the cave, and the echo told them it was not too big. She got out her torch, and they entered nervously, remembering the history of the place; robbers, thieves, and smugglers had lived here long ago. Well, hopefully, long ago.

After a few metres, the cave widened out into a large opening. It was damp and smelt dank and musty, and an unpleasant chill crept into their bones. Carol shone her torch around the walls. They were moist and craggy, at places dripping with water as it seeped through the rock. On the ground, there were remnants of a fire, surrounded by rocks and littered with old beer cans.

Beryl pulled a face.

"Yuck, I wouldn't want to live here."

"Not unless you were hiding and had no choice." Carol shone the torch around the walls to make sure there were no tunnel openings, but she could not see any. The girls left quickly and inhaled deep gulps of fresh air. The cave was depressing, and they did not want to stay there a moment longer.

"How could people live in there? They must have been desperate. Let's check the other tunnels." Beryl cautiously stepped from rock to rock along the cliff face, careful not to slip.

Most of the other tunnels were dead ends, too shallow or narrow, with openings the size of a football or grapefruit. Nevertheless, the girls shone their torches or poked sticks inside, checking every opening thoroughly, though they had a feeling they would find nothing. If there was something hidden inside, someone would have found it before them.

They retreated from the noisy spray and sat on some rocks by the forest edge. They were soaked and glum, and they realised they had to get to the cave behind the falls, and that was daunting. It would not be easy to get to the falls or go behind them. You would have to slide along a dangerously slippery ledge and get drenched. Then you would have to climb into some awful tight tunnel. No wonder the cave behind the falls was unknown, an ideal place for hiding something.

"No choice, Nonco." Carol shuddered. "We have to check behind the falls."

"And that we would be me, I suppose?" Beryl groaned.

"Yep," said Carol sympathetically. "Sorry, but you're the tall, thin Finn."

"You know how I feel about tight places!" Beryl moaned.

"I do, and I'm sorry, but it's you that taught me that courage is being scared and doing it anyway. No guts, no glory."

Beryl knew she had to go.

"Give me some of that chocolate," she bargained.

"Certainly not!" grinned Carol. "Don't want to fatten you up before the mission." But she fished a 'Kit Kat' from her rucksack and gave it all to Beryl without even taking her half.

Beryl munched with deliberation then stood up abruptly and declared, "When the going gets tough…"

"The tough get going." Carol smiled. The chocolate had worked. "Head torch, goggles, and one bottle of Rescue Remedy, ma'am." She pulled the stuff out of her bag and handed the items to Beryl. The goggles and torch would be useful in a dark wet cave, and Rescue Remedy was an excellent flower essence that calmed the nerves in panicky situations, like before exams. If you were ever going on a trip to the Amazon or the moon, Carol would be the person you would want by your side.

Beryl peeled off her clothes. She was wearing her swimsuit underneath. She put on rubber shoes and strapped the goggles over her eyes and the torch onto her head. She tucked the bottle of Rescue Remedy inside her swimsuit, gave Carol the short secret handshake, and walked to the edge of the pool, looking like a frogman and feeling scared. She stepped into the icy cold water, which made her catch her breath, then wadded through the pool towards the edge of the falls. The rocks were slippery, the water freezing, and the spray intense. Carol watched anxiously as Beryl climbed onto the narrow ledge and edged along the cliff until she was beside the falling water. She saw Beryl hesitate for a moment, then she seemed to leap behind the water and was gone.

That was the moment Carol felt a hand on her shoulder.

CHAPTER 32

Beryl looked down at the water crashing onto the rocks below her. She could see the sharp jagged edges protruding from the water like stalagmites. If she slipped and fell on those, she would be impaled. A horrible image flashed through her mind of her lying shattered on the rocks below. No way would she survive. She grasped the nooks in the cliff so tightly that her fingers began to cramp. The spray was smashing into her face, coming on in gushes that felt like hard slaps. She could sense the incredible power of the water and realised that it could easily smash her to bits. This was not the kind of waterfall you sat under to gently massage your scalp. It would probably knock your head off before it massaged it.

Inch by inch, Beryl crept closer to the gap between the cliff and the pouring cascade until she reached the point where the ledge cut off, obviously eroded by the powerful waterfall. The gap between the cliff and the falls was very narrow. Behind the crashing curtain of water, quite a bit higher up, she could just make out the end of the ledge where it continued behind the falls. She would have to make a really big jump to get to it, but Beryl couldn't see if there was a proper foothold or anything to hang onto on the other side. She might jump onto nothing or hit the waterfall, and that would be the end, she would be smashed onto the rocks below. Beryl was terrified of going forward but could not hang onto the cliff much longer. She felt her feet slipping on the watery ledge. Her heart was screaming at her to go back, her mind was pushing her to go on: go for the treasure, go for Carol.

She made the jump.

Beryl must have landed on the ledge because, suddenly, there she was behind the fall, and everything changed. A strange sense of tranquillity enveloped her, like entering the eye of the storm. She could hear the water, but it seemed to come from a distant world. She took a few deep breaths to calm her pounding heart, then continued along the ledge, the water falling almost silently behind her. The ridge was slightly wider, and there were places to hold on to, so she could move along more smoothly. After two or three metres, she found herself in front of the mouth of the cave and, somehow, she knew this was it. The treasure had to be here.

The opening was just under chest height, small and circular, not much larger than a basketball, the size that would admit a child but refuse an adult or youth. A child would not be able to make the jump to behind the falls. A teenager would not fit in. That meant she may fit in and she may not, but it would be very, very tight. No way would Carol fit in here, and Carol was not much larger than Beryl. There was only one way to find out. She switched the head torch on.

Beryl had to decide if to enter with her arms at her sides or in front of her. She needed one hand in front to look for things, so she bent over and tried to enter with one arm in front, and one behind. No go. It was too narrow. She would have to wriggle in with both arms forward. She felt panic rising inside and filling her whole being. There was no way she could do this. Being in an enclosed place made Beryl want to escape, to faint, to die, to scream. She got the bottle of Rescue Remedy out, put a few drops into her mouth, and felt a touch calmer. Then she did some hyperventilating—taking a series of rapid breaths to flood herself with oxygen. It was a trick Carol had taught her when they were swimming underwater at the swimming pool. She counted 100 breaths, bent her head to tunnel level, and pushed herself in arms first. She could just about fit—if she were any bigger, she would be stuck. Beryl imagined Tim and his friends trying to enter. It would have been impossible. She was younger and thinner, and even she could barely squeeze in.

She pushed herself forward with her legs until they left the ground. From here, she would have to wriggle forward. There was nothing to hold on to, but once she entered, she realised the cave was smooth and slippery from water and moss, so she was able to slide forward. The air was stuffy, and she had to breathe slowly through her nose. Her torch beam shone into the darkness, and she realised with horror that the tunnel was deeper than she had imagined—she could not see the end. Using her feet, knees, and elbows, Beryl shuffled forward, grateful for the slippery floor. She felt something stringy with her hand and realised it was a net—someone had tried to fish something out.

She pushed on, inch by inch.

This was Beryl's ultimate nightmare. The walls were closing in on her, she could not move sideways or up and down. Her head grazed the roof of the cave, her elbows were compressed by its sides. It occurred to her that she might get stuck in the narrow cave forever, and she started repeating in her mind, 'I would rather die, I would rather die!' She wanted to scream, to back out, to wriggle, but she could do none of those. Her air was running out. She tried to counter the panic by thinking of something boring, like supermarkets, but the terror rose and gripped her whole being. She tried to reach for the Rescue Remedy, but her arms were stuck in front of her. Her whole body was inside the tunnel, but there was no end in sight. She began retching and felt vomit rising in her throat. Her mind was screaming, 'get out, get out, get out! Now,

now! NOW!' She was about to faint and would be stuck inside, unconscious, and die there. She grabbed for a stone to cling to, but it came loose. It felt strangely square and smooth in her hand.

Then everything went black.

CHAPTER 33

Carol swerved around with a start, her heart beating like a runaway horse. The last thing she expected was someone else to be in the middle of the forest, let alone right behind her. Her eyes met a red and black checkered flannel shirt, and when she looked up, a man was standing in front of her. He was tall with a hard face, unshaven, and peppered with acne scars. He reeked of alcohol and tobacco, and the smell made Carol want to retch. She took two steps backwards but stumbled on a rock and lost her balance for a moment.

"Calm down, little girl." His tone was threatening.

Carol felt a lump blocking her throat, she was gulping for air and couldn't make a sound.

"No need to be scared, girly." He tried to put on a kind voice, though this was clearly not his natural tone.

"What do you want?" Carol tried to back away again without tripping on the rocks. "Why did you sneak up on me?" Her voice was trembling.

"Sneak up?" He shook his head. "No, girly, I was just walking by 'ere, see, and I heard some sounds and come to look, see." His accent was northern, Yorkshire probably. "I know everyone wot comes in an' out of me forest, see, lived here all me life. Where's your friend then?"

"Friend? W... w... w... what friend?" Carol's heart sank when

116

he pointed at the two bikes lying on the grass. "Er… we're playing hide and seek."

"Well, if you're looking for her, my guess is that she's over there." He pointed to the falls. "And perhaps she is doing some hide and seeking herself? Like looking in the cave perhaps?"

Carol's heart missed two beats. Her lungs seized, and she was fighting for air. He obviously knew something. Her mind was racing. How could she escape? Should she run? But where was Beryl? She had to stay for Beryl. How could she warn her?

"I've no idea what you are talking about." Carol backed away, but she was now at the edge of the thick forest and couldn't go further. She had to do something. What do you do in these situations? What did Dad teach her, what did Jerry say?

"If you come one more step towards me, I'm going to scream so loud they will hear me in town."

"Ain't coming near you, girly, see?" He opened his hands as if to show her he wasn't armed. He wouldn't have to be, thought Carol, he could flatten me with one blow. She wanted to run into the woods. But Beryl…where was she?

"Well, we just gonna sit 'ere together and wait for your friend and see if she found something." He sat on a rock facing the falls, pulled out a packet of cheap cigarettes and lit one, blowing the smoke in Carol's direction.

Carol stood as far away as she could, ready to run, but at the same time frantically searching her mind for a way out. How could she warn Beryl? And what was happening with her anyway? She had been gone for way too long. The cave couldn't be that big. She tried to calm her breathing, but her mind was out of control. From the corner of her eye, she was looking at the falls. Come on Beryl! Come on!! No, don't come on. Stay hidden. This was bad. She had to help her friend, but the man…. She had to do something, to be smart, to use girl power.

They sat and waited. The seconds ticked like years.

"Maybe she found something there wot belong to me." He puffed more smoke at Carol. She screwed up her face.

"If there is something there wot belong to you," Carol mimicked his accent, "how come you don't get it yourself?"

"Well, now, that's 'cause it's difficult for me to get in there, see."

"Well, if it's difficult for you to get in there, see, how did you put it there in the first place, see?" Carol wagged her head in ridicule, getting some satisfaction from the puzzled look on his face.

"Don't ask too many questions," he snarled and flicked his cigarette butt into the rocks.

Just then, Carol saw Beryl's shadow move behind the falls.

"Maria!" She cupped her hands and shouted as loudly as she could so that Beryl could hear her above the noise of the falls. "Are you okay? Come out, Maria, we can't play hide and seek anymore, there's a nasty man here with some funny ideas."

"Yeah, come on out, Maria," shouted the man.

A long moment passed before Beryl came out. Carol held her breath. Finally, Beryl appeared from behind the curtain of water, made a large leap to the ledge, edged her way slowly along the ridge and waded through the pool. She looked pale and unwell as if she had seen a ghost. She was carrying nothing in her hands and had lost the torch and goggles. Carol was even more worried. What had happened to Beryl? She looked awful! At least she didn't have the treasure, nothing for this man to take from them.

"Come on up here, Maria." The man tried to put on his friendly voice again. "Got something on you?"

Carol could see Beryl was hardly able to walk.

"Leave her alone!" She went over to help Beryl.

"Just checking she doesn't have my stuff!" He looked Beryl up and down. "You find anything there, Maria?"

Beryl was breathing hard but getting some colour back.

"I don't know what you are talking about, mister. You can see very well I just have my swimming costume on." She raised her arms and opened her palms, then spun around. "Just water and rock back there. We were playing hide and seek."

The man looked puzzled and disappointed.

"Did you go into that tunnel, Maria?" he asked.

"Are you kidding?!" Beryl was getting her spunk back. "Do you seriously think I could fit in there, or that I would go down that hole even if I could? Anyway, none of your business, mister, and if you carry on bothering us, we're both going to scream so loud they will hear us in town."

This time he was up against two girls rather than one, so he hesitated.

"Sure you ain't got nothing there, Maria?" He took a step towards Beryl.

Carol opened her mouth and screamed so loudly that they probably could hear her in town, and she didn't stop for a whole minute. Her scream was so ear-piercing it could have shattered glass, and it went on and on and on. Even Beryl was finding it hard to take. But Carol continued blaring, gulping for air, and then screaming louder and louder.

The man was startled and took two steps back.

"Now, now, girlies," he said, raising his hands as if Carol was pointing a gun at him. "No need to do that." Men hated screaming kids.

"Would you like to hear us screaming together, mister?" asked Beryl. "We're very good at it."

The man shook his head in alarm and muttered something like, "No, no."

"Then come on, Judith." Beryl picked up her bike. "Let's get the heck out of here."

Beryl jumped on her bike, still in her wet swimsuit. Carol

grabbed the two rucksacks and got her bike, and before the man had time to recover, they were gone.

CHAPTER 34

T he girls peddled faster than they had ever peddled before, ignoring the roots and bumps on their path. They kept going for a long time without talking or stopping. They rode past the second falls, past the first falls, all the way back to the camp, past a snoring George, and into the bike shed, where they dumped their bicycles and made for their tent. When they were inside, they lay on their sleeping bags gasping, too breathless and frightened to talk. Their hearts were beating from the intense ride, but more so from the fear they had both experienced. Finally, Beryl fished out the Aconite bottle from her first aid kit, and they each took a couple of little pellets and calmed down. Aconite was an excellent remedy for fright. Beryl changed out of her swimming costume, Carol dished out some chocolate cookies, and they were finally relaxed enough to talk.

"Are you okay?" asked Carol with concern. "You looked like you were going to faint back there."

"Correction, Nonco, I had already fainted," replied Beryl.

"You fainted?" Carol was alarmed. "Where? How?"

"In the tunnel," said Beryl, "and don't you ever make me go in there again."

"I won't, I won't," Carol promised. "So sorry! How long were you out for?"

"I honestly don't know," replied Beryl. "The tunnel was much deeper than I thought. I was in with my whole body and with my arms in front of me, so I couldn't move. I panicked and had to get out. The next thing I knew, I blacked out. But, luckily for me my face fell into the water, and it woke me up. I think I was probably out for 30 seconds."

"Oh my God." Carol was incredibly upset. "Thank goodness you made it out! It was just after you went in that the creep appeared. I was so worried, but I couldn't come to look for you."

"Yes, the creep!" echoed Beryl. "Tell me about him."

Carol told her how the man suddenly appeared from behind her, and how he knew there was something of value in the tunnel, and how he made her wait for Beryl with him.

"Thank goodness you found nothing." She meant it, but her tone was disappointed. "He would have just taken it from us. Well," she sighed, "I suppose that's the end of our treasure hunt. Dead end."

Beryl was silent for a long moment.

Then she said in a slow, deliberate tone, "Listen up, Nonco. Who said I found nothing?"

It was Carol's turn to be a fish. She opened and closed her mouth several times, but nothing came out. Beryl sat waiting, a slight grin on her lips.

"But... but, you mean, but, but you had nothing..." Carol managed to stutter.

"That's right, dear Judith," Beryl said smugly. "Maria had nothing, but Beryl did."

For many years, the girls had used their middle names, Maria and Judith, in an emergency or when they wanted to signal that something was wrong. Beryl had almost been called Maria after her mother, but at the last minute her mum had chosen Beryl, thinking it rhymed with her best friend Naomi's new baby, Carol. So, 'Beryl Maria' it was. Beryl was mad at her mother for giving her a weird name until she was six years old, but since she found out that Beryl meant a green precious stone, she liked it.

"When I came out of the tunnel, I had a strange slab of stone in my hand," Beryl explained. "It was square and smooth. I don't remember how it got there. I think I might've grabbed onto it when I panicked. There was nothing on one side, but the other side had a map engraved on it. I was just looking at it when I heard you call Maria, and I knew something was wrong. So, I hid it in one of the little holes in the cliff face and came out."

"We have a map!?" Carol was thrilled. "Unbelievable!"

"Technically we *will* have a map," corrected Beryl, pleased to finally be the one with more information. "Once we go back and get it."

Carol groaned as it dawned on her that they would have to make the journey to the falls and risk seeing the man again. Still, they had made a big step forward in their quest. They had a map!

"Did you manage to see what was on it?" Carol asked.

"No," replied Beryl. "All I saw was a picture of a house and a tree, and some writing, but I didn't have time to check it out properly. Why do you think whoever made the map engraved it on stone and not paper?"

Carol thought for a while. "Paper wouldn't have lasted in such a damp place."

"Makes sense." Beryl nodded. "But that means they knew it would be there for a long time."

"Right," Carol said slowly, thinking again. "Maybe they couldn't sell whatever they had because it was stolen or something like that. And they were hiding."

The girls were silent for a while.

Then Beryl asked, "Go back today or tomorrow?'

"We're way too tired to go today. Let's check with Mr. Phillips and see if the bikes are available tomorrow," said Carol. They were both dreading the trip back, but it had to be done.

They walked over to Mr. Phillips's office. They were just about to knock on the door when Carol grabbed Beryl's hand and pulled her back sharply. Beryl looked at her in surprise, and then she heard it too.

The man in the red checkered shirt was in Mr. Phillips's office.

CHAPTER 35

"**M**aria and Judith was their names." They could hear the man's northern accent. "All I want is to give them back their torch, see."

The girls hid back behind the door, trying to hear but being very careful not to move.

"I told you once already, Hank," Mr. Phillips was saying, "there is no Maria or Judith here. There are no girls here at all, and no one took the bikes out today. So, you have it wrong. Why not try Eden Valley camp down the road. Probably came from there."

"You sure, Les?" Hank asked again.

"I am telling you one last time, Hank." Mr. Phillips raised his voice. "No Maria, no Judith, no girls, no bikes. Now listen carefully, Hank, because I will say this just once. If I catch you bothering anyone in my camp, I will call the police. It won't take much to get you back inside, seeing as you're out of prison on probation."

The girls shrunk further back when they heard that.

"No need for that, Les," said Hank, sounding alarmed. "I'll go down to Eden camp and see if they're there. All I want is to give them back their torch, see."

"Oh, I'm sure you do, Hank," Mr. Phillips said in a mocking tone. "Now be off, and don't let me see you here again."

The girls backed away silently, retreating behind Mr. Phillips's office to the safety of the girls' showers. Carol went to the little window and looked out.

"He's checking out the tents," she said, and then after a while, "Okay, he's gone. No car, he walked down the road in the opposite direction, probably towards Eden."

"Then we have to go now, quick," Beryl urged, "while we know where he is. We might not be so sure tomorrow."

Carol groaned, but Beryl was right. Both girls were utterly exhausted from the morning bike ride, but they had no choice. They agreed it was best not to see Mr. Phillips before they left, so they went back to the bike shed, took the bikes, and snuck out past a snoring George.

* * *

This time, the bike ride was awful. The girls had already ridden twenty-four miles there and back, and it had taken over four hours. It was now 2:30 PM, so they could be home by 7:00 PM if all went well. Fortunately, they were both fit from basketball and swimming, so they passed the second falls in just over an hour and a half, and forty-five minutes later they could hear the large falls. The girls were nervous. Could Hank have somehow got back to the falls before them? They had seen him walk off in the other direction, but he may have turned around and come back, or perhaps someone else was waiting there. They stopped about a hundred metres away and hid their bikes in the forest, then crept silently through the woods, stopping now and again to listen for suspicious sounds. When they reached the edge of the trees, they crouched behind some bushes and watched for five minutes to make sure no one was there. The coast seemed clear.

"Okay," said Beryl, "it's got to be me. You wait here." She didn't have her swimming costume with her, so she was going to get wet.

"Be careful, good luck!" Carol said. "If I see anything, I'll do our whistle, and if you don't hear that, I'll scream Maria."

"Okay, Judith," Beryl said nervously. She looked around one more time then exited the forest, ran to the falls, took off her shoes, and waded into the pool below. A few moments later, she was behind the waterfall. Carol held her breath. It felt like an hour, but it was only a minute or two before Beryl reappeared. Carol could see she was holding something.

"Run, Beryl, run," Carol whispered to herself. Beryl ran, and a moment later, she was next to Carol, soaked and panting.

"Got it." She showed Carol the stone proudly. They retreated into the woods then crouched down to examine the stone. It was square, about the size of a small bathroom tile, perhaps some kind of limestone. Carol saw the picture of a house and tree etched on it. She peered closer at the faint engraving. There was writing, but she could not make the letters out.

"Let's get out of here." Carol wrapped the stone in her hat and put it in her rucksack. They were anxious about Hank coming back, so they did not take time to rest. The girls got on their bikes and rode off as quickly as they could.

The journey back was tough. Neither of the girls had ridden a bike so far in one day, and they were physically and emotionally exhausted and now dying of hunger. Their legs felt as if they would fall off, their hands were cramping, their muscles were burning, their backs were screaming. Every peddle push was an ordeal, but they had to keep going. By 7:30 PM they were nearing the camp. Just as they arrived at the gate, they met Mr. Phillips on his way home. He stopped his car and opened the window.

"Hello, girls." He smiled but looked concerned. "Maria and Judith, if I'm not mistaken?"

Beryl and Carol looked at each other awkwardly. Then Beryl nodded.

"Aye, aye, sir, that's us."

They laughed, but then Mr. Phillips was serious again.

"Listen, girls. I understand Hank Jackson met you and bothered you. I am very sorry about that. His bark is worse than his bite, but he is obsessed with some ridiculous treasure he thinks is hidden in the caves. Funnily enough, Tim had the same idea, but I never believed that kind of rubbish. Anyway, I told Hank that I don't know you, and warned him to keep away from the camp. I have informed George not to let him in under any circumstances, so you are perfectly safe. He knows that if he makes any trouble, we will call the police. Do you feel okay about that?"

Beryl nodded again. "That sounds fine, Mr. Phillips. To be honest, he did scare us at the falls, and we were nervous about coming back here, which is why we are so late."

"I'm so sorry, girls. I'm sure there will be no more trouble. George will call me if there is. Meanwhile, you can feel as safe as houses."

I'd feel safer in our own little house, Beryl thought, but said, "Yes, sir, safe as tents."

The girls walked back to the tent. They were hurting all over, and it was clear they would not get to their Meukki that night, either. Carol got the map out and hid it in a tent pocket. Then she covered it with dirty socks to put anyone off from looking. They felt too tired to move or cook, but they hadn't eaten since breakfast, so Beryl fetched some readymade food from the camp fridge while Carol got the stove going. They sat waiting for the food to warm up, too exhausted to talk, but both thinking the same thing. They had found it! They had found the map to the treasure, and this was the most exciting thing that had ever happened to them.

The food was nearly ready when they heard angry shouting from the gate.

CHAPTER 36

The girls peered over the tent and saw George's broad back blocking someone at the gate. He was waving his hands and pushing someone. Then they heard the other voice. It was Hank. The girls' blood ran cold.

They could overhear Hank shouting, "Let me in George, or I'll let myself in, see!"

By this time, the other campers were standing outside their tents looking at the scene with evident surprise. No one knew what to make of it, except the two girls.

They heard George shouting, "I'll have the police on you, Hank," and Hank replying, "You go ahead, George. Meanwhile, you show me where this Maria's tent is." The girls looked at each other with dread.

Carol quickly turned the stove off and hid the cooking utensils, while Beryl threw all their stuff in the tent and zipped the door. They switched off the lantern torch. Thankfully they were far from the main camp lights, so it was now getting dark. The girls huddled behind the tent, hoping Hank would leave. Suddenly they heard a cry of pain from the gate. They peeked from behind the tent and saw George lying on the grass, holding his jaw.

Hank had marched off to the first tent on the far side of the field and was shouting, "Maria, come out, I have your torch!" The campers were running to their tents in alarm. It did not seem that there was anyone strong or brave enough to confront Hank.

"Time to get out of here," Beryl whispered, "let's go!"

Crouching low, the two girls headed for the hole in the fence. Beryl held the flap open while Carol crawled through, then wriggled through herself. Carol closed the flap so their gate could not be seen. They crawled on all fours towards the river path. The ground was stony and hard, so their palms and knees were getting scratched and bruised, but they kept going.

They could hear Hank coming closer to their tent, all the time shouting, "Maria, Judith!" There were a few responses from the tents saying, "There's no Maria or Judith here, go away," but they were meek.

They reckoned Hank was about five or six tents away when Beryl grabbed Carol's ankle and whispered, "The Map!" with urgency in her voice.

Carol stopped moving, and Beryl heard her take in a sharp gasp of air. Then she turned to her friend and whispered, "I'm going back. If he finds it, he will get to the treasure first."

"I'll go," said Beryl.

"You've done your share for today." And before Beryl could stop her, Carol had risen and started to run in a low crouch towards the fence. She opened the flap and crawled through, then closed it again. Hank was arguing with some people two tents down, and from his slurry speech she knew he was drunk.

Carol crawled on all fours towards the tent. She was so pumped with fear that she could hardly feel her jeans tearing and her knees scratching on the stones. Carol unzipped the tent flap, snuck inside, and grabbed the stone map from the tent pocket. She rolled out of the tent, zipped the flap, and began crawling toward the hole in the fence when suddenly there were two large legs in blue jeans standing in front of her.

"Hello, Judith," said Hank. "Going somewhere?"

Carol did what she was trained to do in this kind of situation. She screamed. She screamed so loudly that she thought her own eardrum would blow. Hank took two steps back in alarm. Carol carried on screaming but seized the opportunity to get up and run past Hank towards the fence. But Hank was quick. He reached out his enormous hand and caught Carol's shirt sleeve, spinning her around. She gasped in fear, holding on to the stone so tightly that she cut her hand.

"Come here, girly," Hank growled in a nasty voice. "Do you have something for me?"

He pulled Carol towards him, and she pressed the stone-hard into her stomach, wishing she could swallow it through there. She could smell the alcohol and tobacco on his breath. People from the camp were gathering around the tent after Carol's terrifying scream, shouting to Hank to let her go. One elderly man rushed in and tried to pull her free, but Hank punched him in the face with his free arm, and he went reeling to the ground. Everyone else took a step back in alarm.

"Give it here, girly," snarled Hank, "and I'll let you go. Otherwise, you gonna get a right smacking, see!" He raised his hand menacingly. Carol deliberately fell on the ground and curled into a ball, clutching the stone tightly to her chest. He began pulling her up, and she knew all was lost. He would get the map.

"Judith! Here, here!" came Beryl's voice from across the fence.

Beryl sounded just like she did in a basketball game when she wanted someone to pass her the ball, and Carol got the message immediately. Just as Hank pulled her upright, she lobbed the stone over the fence and into Beryl's waiting arms. Beryl had no trouble catching it, because that's what basketball players do. As soon as Hank saw the stone sail over the fence and into Beryl's hands, he let go of Carol and rushed towards Beryl, but in the dark, he didn't see the fence. He ran straight into it and must have got barbed wire in his face because he screamed and clutched his eye.

Beryl turned and ran towards the river and was swallowed by the dark. Carol didn't hang around either. She turned and ran through the crowd towards the safety of the girls' showers. Hank hesitated. He didn't know whether to chase Carol or to follow Beryl into the woods. After a few seconds, Hank decided to go after Beryl, but could not work out how to get over the fence. He turned back to look for Carol, but she was gone, so he let off a cry of rage which sounded like a wounded animal. Everyone took another step backwards, and it was then that they heard the police siren.

Hank looked around, desperate for a way out, but there was none. He only had two or three minutes to escape the camp and get lost in the forest. He ran to the gate and was about to get through it when George stepped out in front of him holding a large cricket bat in his hand.

"Stand back, Hank," he said calmly, "or I will split your head in two."

Hank took a step back, frantically looking for another way out. That was the moment the police car arrived at the gate, followed closely by Mr. Phillips's car.

CHAPTER 37

M r. and Mrs. Phillips sat in the office facing the two girls, who were both now wrapped in blankets and sipping hot chocolate. No doubt they were in shock, but the hot chocolate was seeping into their stomachs and bones and warming them up.

"Some more cookies, girls?" asked Mrs. Phillips in a concerned, motherly voice. "More hot chocolate?"

Both girls nodded, too tired and shaken to say a word.

"I am so very, very sorry that this happened," Mrs. Phillips repeated for the eleventh time. "You are both very brave girls! We've been running this campsite for twelve years, and we've never had anything like this happen. I simply cannot understand what came over Hank. I know he can drink, but he's not usually aggressive. What did he want from you?"

Beryl thought that a half-truth was better than an outright lie.

"He met us at the large falls and kept going on about some treasure he thought we had."

Mr. Phillips looked at his wife then sat back and sighed, a look of understanding spreading across his face.

"Now I get the picture. Let me explain." He folded his fingers, lost in thought for a moment.

"When Tim and I were about sixteen, just after I got my first job at this campsite, Tim used to stop by when he was hiking and camp here. We often sat by the campfire talking all night. Tim loved the forest, and he knew every trail, river, and cave. But he was a big reader too, and he studied history, geography, and geology, so he was always teaching me things. He loved adventure books as well, mainly about smugglers or pirates. Anyway, Hank was a couple of years older than us, also in the boy scouts, and we used to hang out with him occasionally. Hank was a decent chap at the time. Annie was around too. She had a crush on Tim but, after Tim vanished, Hank and Annie started going out and eventually got married. But after a few years, she left him, and he has never been the same since."

He poured them another hot chocolate from the pot.

"Anyway, as I said, Tim, Hank, and I used to hang out and hike together. Then one day, Tim comes up with this story. He read some book about lost treasures and somehow worked out that a stolen treasure was smuggled from Ireland and hidden in the caves by the falls. He had studied the whole subject carefully, as he always did. No one else knew about this, except the thief or robbers themselves. No way anyone else could have worked it out, but Tim, with his clever brain and vast knowledge, put two and two together and realised it had to be in this area. He reckoned that the treasure was well known, so the thief couldn't sell it, and that detectives from all over the country were after him. The thief would have had no option but to escape, hide himself and the loot, and Tim worked out the most likely path he would have followed. He even hiked it himself. Took three days but he did it. Clever boy that Tim was, hardly ever wrong, and when he had a problem, he would go to any lengths to solve it."

Mr. Phillips paused for a moment, deep in thought. The girls were sitting on the edge of their seats, drinking up every word; the excitement was warming them more than the hot chocolate.

"Well, to cut a long story short," Mr. Phillips continued. At this point, the girls didn't want him to cut the story short, but they didn't want to interrupt him either, so they just listened. "Tim went on and on about this treasure. Wouldn't say what it was though, even though we urged him to—said that that was his secret and that if anyone ever got an inkling about it, the whole place would be full of police and detectives. I usually believed just about anything Tim said because he was a sensible chap and could always back himself up, but I found this one a stretch. I mean, let's be realistic, girls. The thief or thieves could have chosen so many paths and places to hide.

"But Hank bought Tim's story big time, he was always looking for adventure and quick money. They used to sit and discuss it for hours, studying maps and books and different routes that the thief could have taken. They weren't sure, but they had a theory that the thief hid in the cave by the big falls because that was a well-known hiding place for rascals and fugitives for hundreds of years.

Tim and Hank reckoned the thief might have hidden the treasure nearby, perhaps in one of the smaller caves. They explored every cave in the area except for one, the cave behind the falls. Not sure if you girls got to see it. It was too small to get inside and very deep. You needed a child or a thin teenager to slide inside, but a child would never be able to make the dangerous jump to behind the falls. They kept looking for the right person, but they couldn't find anyone tall and old enough to jump but thin enough to get in the cave. They would have found someone eventually, but then Tim vanished, and that was the end of that."

Mr. Phillips paused. For a moment, he glanced at Beryl, and the girls could see he was wondering about her long thin body.

"Please carry on, Mr. Phillips," Carol urged, pulling his attention away from her friend.

Mr. Phillips continued. "After Tim vanished, Hank enlisted in the army. When he finished his service, he married Annie and forgot about the treasure. But the company Hank worked for went bust, he got into debt and hit the bottle, so after a couple of years, Annie left him. Next thing you know, he robbed a post office and spent four years in jail. Big shame really, he was a good chap and could have been much more. I guess Tim vanishing and Annie leaving were too much for him. I had no idea he was still looking for the treasure. I guess he thinks he could use the money to get Annie back."

The girls felt a slight pang of sorrow for Hank and his sad story, but what had happened that day was too fresh in their minds to allow for much sympathy.

"Anyway, this is all over now, and you are totally safe." Mrs. Phillips said gravely. "Hank was on probation so he will probably get a prison sentence for entering the campsite and behaving violently. I hope you decide to finish your holiday here. I have given all the current campers a week's stay for free. As for you, we will never charge you to stay here again. You have a lifelong membership"

"Wow, thanks, Mrs. Phillips." Beryl was genuinely happy. She turned to Mr. Phillips. "But do you think that perhaps it would be best not to tell our parents about this? They would never let us come again."

Mr. Phillips pretended to think, but they could see he was relieved about this suggestion. He looked at his wife again, and she gave him a slight nod.

After a moment, Mr. Phillips declared, as though he had finally come to a difficult decision, "Good thinking," he said. "If word of this gets out, the campsite is finished. This is our family business, and of course I don't want to frighten your families either." He looked at them with a plea in his eyes. "Are you sure you're happy to keep this story to yourselves?"

Beryl and Carol looked at each other and nodded. They didn't need their families asking awkward questions either.

"Our lips are sealed, Mr. Phillips. We understand and will not tell anyone," Carol promised. "But we have one request." Beryl looked at her with surprise. Carol went on. "You understand that we're both shaken and need a few days to recover. We want to stay until the end of our holiday, and if we go home now, our parents will want to know why. But honestly, Mr. Phillips, we're too scared to sleep here at night. Would you mind if we spent the rest of our holiday at our friend's house down the road? I'm sure they would love to have us, and we can tell our parents we just wanted to visit them. That way, no one has to know anything." Carol could see a grin tickling the edge of Beryl's mouth, but she kept looking at Mr. Phillips. He thought for a moment.

"Sure thing, girls," he said eventually, "and thanks for understanding."

Carol and Beryl stood up.

"Thank you for the life membership, Mrs. Phillips," said Carol.

"You'll be seeing a lot more of us from now on."

They said goodnight and turned to go, but just before they left, Mr. Phillips said, "Excuse me, Judith and Maria, but are you sure you never found any treasure?" He had a twinkle in his eye.

"No, sir," replied Maria with a smile. "Nothing of the sort."

CHAPTER 38

The girls slept in their tent simply because they were too tired and sore to move an inch. After cycling to the falls and back twice in one day, and the scene with Hank, they were exhausted. They lay on top of their sleeping bags, fully clothed and didn't wake up until eleven o'clock the next morning. It was only then that they noticed that they were hurting all over. Scraped knees and elbows, aching muscles and torn jeans were testimonies to the previous day's adventure. So, Beryl dished out some Arnica, the best medicine for aches and bruises, and they both went for a long, hot shower followed by an egg, salmon, and avocado brunch, after which they felt much better.

No doubt they still carried some emotional shock, but that had been soothed by Mr. Phillips's story. Hank was gone, and good old Tim had been proved right. And it was them, and only them, who had carried his mission through. This gave the two girls a great sense of satisfaction.

"That Tim was something else," said Beryl. "He worked the whole thing out by himself. Imagine, he reads about the treasure in the book, then puts himself in the thief's shoes and works out exactly where they were, what they were thinking and how they had to act. Then he walks the talk and follows their tracks. And incredibly, he was proved right where none of the detectives could solve it."

"That's right, but Tim could never have done it without you."

Carol looked at her friend with appreciation.

This was true. If Beryl had been six months younger and not a basketball player, she would never have been able to make the jump behind the falls. If she had been six months older, she would not have been able to enter the cave. Beryl was the unique, time sensitive key to the waterfall's lock. Only she could retrieve the map.

Then a thought occurred to Carol. If Beryl was the key, who was the lock? If Beryl's unique age and physique allowed her to jump the falls and crawl into the cave, the thief's physique had to be similar; tall, thin, athletic, and young.

And possibly female.

She told Beryl.

"Maybe the thief was a big man, and he just threw the map into the cave?" Beryl countered.

"If that was the case, he must have known someone with a similar build to you to fish it out. By the way, where is the map?" Carol asked suddenly, remembering the night before.

"Don't worry, Nonco," Beryl laughed. "Safe and soundly hidden by clever old Beryl. Mind you, that was a pretty good throw yesterday. You should be playing basketball, Dame Peril!"

They sat and chatted about yesterday's events for a while, then washed the dishes and tidied the tent. When they were done, they went over to talk to George.

"Hello, girls," he said with an embarrassed smile. "So very sorry about last night. I should have been able to stop him." The girls noticed he had a big bruise on his cheek.

"That's okay, George," said Beryl kindly. "After all, it was you that stopped him from escaping. Didn't know you could play cricket!" She swung an air bat.

George perked up.

"Used to be quite the batsman in my day," he said proudly. "Anyway, Mr. Phillips tells me you will be staying with friends for a while. I understand."

"That's right," said Beryl. "But we are leaving our stuff here and will come and visit."

Beryl and Carol phoned their parents to assure them all was well. They took food supplies from the fridge, got everything they needed from the tent, slipped through the hole in the fence, and walked off towards their beloved Meukki and three days of bliss.

On the way to the bridge, Beryl stopped by a large oak, crouched down, and retrieved the stone map from where she had quickly hidden it last night before she ran back to help Carol.

The girls crossed the bridge and walked down the path to the clearing. As soon as they arrived, they relaxed, as beautiful nature sucked all the tension out of their tired minds and bodies and dumped it deep under the ground. The clearing looked magnificent in the summer light, covered with grass and delicate summer flowers. The oak stood tall and in full leaf, its giant canopy shading a large part of the clearing, and under it nestled their little house, cosy and inviting. It was perfect, and for the first time, they had three days and two nights of pure home time. No parents, no brothers, no bully boys, no school or maths or sport, no Mrs. Phillips or George checking on them. Just pure home! They threw down their bags and lay on the grass, enjoying the feeling of earth and tree and sky for a long time before they spoke.

"I've got big plans for these three days," said Carol. "Like doing lots of nothing!"

"Perhaps some minor activities, like sleeping?" Beryl suggested.

"Hmm, yes, and perhaps eating, lots of food left."

"Reading, swimming, games, campfire, eating, and more sleeping."

"Whoa, that's getting to be a bit full on! I'm here to relax."

"Only one bit at a time, of course," Beryl laughed.

And that is precisely what they did. Lots of nothing interspersed with bursts of more nothing and the occasional activity so that they could rest again afterwards. There was one thing they did do, which was to tie a long rope from the oak and attach a wooden plank to the bottom. This made an excellent river swing. The girls would sit or stand on the plank and go for a running jump, letting go in the middle of the river and landing with a splash. The river was now lazy and warm, perfect for swimming in on the hot summer days. They read books, played Frisbee, cards, chess, and backgammon.

In the evenings they sat by the campfire, watching the flames dance their light around the clearing. When the embers were warm, they wrapped potatoes in silver foil and buried them in the bottom of the fire, where they baked into a late-night snack. Then they retired for a hot chocolate and a last game in their little house, sitting around the table they had built and enjoying the warm, cosy feeling of wood and rug. They felt completely safe, their sleep was deep and refreshing, and their mornings late and lazy.

And so, the three days passed in a dream, and they could have spent much more, but their parents would be coming by to pick them up Saturday afternoon. They missed their families but didn't feel quite ready to go home.

There was one thing they had not done until that last morning, and that was to discuss the treasure or look at the map. It was only after everything was packed and cleaned on Saturday morning that Carol got the stone map out. They took it to Tim's shrine and sat on the log. Rosa, as she was now called, was sprouting new buds from her stem.

"Here's your map, Tim," said Beryl as if talking to an old friend.

"Thanks to you, we found it. You were right all along, and you will get your cut!" said Carol.

Carol placed the map on top of Tim's log, and for the first time, they studied it closely. The engravings were fine and difficult to see clearly, and it was obvious the stone had been subjected to

the ravages of time, weather, and water. The left side was in better
shape than the right, clearly showing a drawing of a church because
of its steep roof with a cross on top. Next to it stood a tree, with
an arrow pointing to the base of its trunk. The tree looked large in
proportion to the church. But the right side of the map had suffered
worse erosion. When they looked closely, the girls could just about
detect some writing, but it was faint, and they couldn't make out
what was written. They tried looking from every angle but could
hardly read a thing.

The girls were overcome with despair. After all this time and
effort, they could not read the map. A church and a tree were
meaningless; there were a thousand places like that in their county.

"My God," said Beryl with frustration. "What the heck are we
going to do now?"

"Perhaps we can take it to some kind of professional person?"

"And then the professional person will go after the treasure,
Nonco."

The girls sat on the ground, deep in thought. It was a dead end.
They could not read the map, and they could not show it to anyone.

"What would you do, Tim?" Beryl spoke to Tim's log. "You
would find a way."

The log said nothing.

They stared at the log with all their might and tried to commu-
nicate with Tim, but there was no response.

Carol levelled the earth with her hand, then took a twig and
drew a church and tree similar to the map. They stared at that for a
while, but it didn't help. In exasperation, she rubbed out the drawing
with her fingers, flattening the earth back into a blank canvas. Dead
end again. She clapped her hands together to get rid of the dirt and
then examined her dirty palms and fingers. Her fingerprints showed
up clearly where the earth had buried itself into their furrows.

She looked at them for a while with fascination and then

declared with a big smile, "Thank you, Tim!"

Beryl looked at her with surprise. "Huh? Are you feeling okay in the head, Peril?"

Carol beamed and showed Beryl her dirty palms and fingers. Beryl looked puzzled and started to say, "Yes, Nonco, you can wash…" Then she stopped mid-sentence and clapped her hands. "Thanks, Tim! You're a genius!"

Carol took the stone, turned it face down, and gently rubbed it into the earth with slow circular movements. Then she turned it over and blew the extra dirt off. They peered at the stone map with renewed excitement. Like invisible ink that had just become visible, the map clearly showed some letters on its surface.

CHAPTER 39

The map was sharper now, the dark earth highlighting the letters and providing a contrast to the pale stone slab. The church stood out clearly, with a large cross in front and a tall window they had not noticed before. The tree had more branches and a thick trunk. The arrow was starker and seemed to point to a dark opening at the base of the trunk. On the right, they could make out some writing, but only a few letters were clear, more to the centre than to the eroded right side. It read 'CHURCH OF C_ R _ _ _ _' and below it the letters 'OL_ _ Y.'

The girls sat silently for a while gazing at the map and the letters, trying to work out what was written. There was an improvement, but it was still going to be difficult.

"Church of Catherine." Beryl was good at this kind of game because she did crossword puzzles and played scrabble.

"Maybe." Carol was not convinced. "The R in Catherine seems too far away."

"Hmmm. R too far away, and wrong word order."

"Calvary," Carol ventured. "…. Nope, R too far again."

"Okay." Beryl kept trying. "R in the third or fourth place." She wrote C_ R and C_ _R in the earth with a twig.

"St. Caroline." Beryl was in full crossword mode now.

"No St. here, and I'm not sure there was a St. Caroline," said Carol, though she liked the idea of a saint with her name.

Beryl looked at the sand, playing with various letter permutations.

"Got it!" she exclaimed suddenly. "So easy—it's Church of Christ!"

"That sounds good!" Carol perked up. "C and R in the right places."

They felt satisfied with that, so they moved on to the next part of the riddle. Beryl wrote with her twig in the ground: OL_ _ Y_ _ _. It wasn't clear how many letters were between the O and Y, and how many after the Y, but they started trying various combinations. They went through 'Oily,' 'Oldy,' 'Only,' and 'Owly' but nothing made sense, so after 15 minutes they gave up.

"It's nearly 11:00 AM. Better get back to the camp," said Carol. "Our parents are coming this afternoon, and we have to pack our camping gear."

They didn't want to take the stone map home, so Carol took a few photos of it, each time rubbing it in the earth again. When she was finished, Beryl wrapped the map tightly in a plastic bag and hid it under a bush at the edge of the clearing that they both knew well. Then they collected their stuff, closed doors and windows, said goodbye to their beloved home, and walked over the bridge to the camp.

CHAPTER 40

It was good to be home with parents and families, but not for long. After a week in nature, their houses seemed cramped and small, the noise from the TV more irritating than usual. Avoiding siblings and Lego was tiring, and having parents supervise your life was stifling. The girls felt like strangers in their own homes, perhaps even slightly superior, as if everything had changed. Still, they realised it was themselves that had changed and not their familiar surroundings. They loved their families, but for the moment they felt like aliens from a distant planet.

As soon as they were allowed out after two days of family time, they retreated to Mrs. E's back garden and sat by the river. It was the closest they could get to their reality.

"I can't stand this much longer," groaned Beryl. "I hid in my room and worked on the puzzle. There are few other church names, but nothing with the letter R in the right place. As for the other word, the best I can find is 'Oldy,' but it doesn't make sense."

Carol took out her notebook. "I also played with the letters but came up empty. So, I looked for 'Church of Christ' on my dad's internet and only found one in our county. It's close enough to bike to."

The treasure hunt was turning out to be much more complicated than they expected, but then, that's what treasure hunts are about.

"If it were easy, someone else would have found it already," said Beryl, "so let's just be grateful it's hard."

"That's the spirit," said Carol. "So how about a trip tomorrow?"

* * *

They informed their parents they were going for a bike ride and received long lectures about road safety. After faithfully promising they would be careful, they loaded day bags and set off to visit the Church of Christ, about 17 miles away. The road was flat and easy compared to the rough, muddy journey of their last ride, so they got to the Church in just over an hour.

It was an old church, dating back to the 18th century. They could see the edge of a graveyard and garden, but they were tucked away behind the church, and when they tried to open the gate, it was locked. The sign read, 'Church of Christ. Open on Sundays, 10:00 AM. All Welcome in the name of the Lord.'

"Darn!" said Beryl, stamping her foot in frustration. "All this way for nothing. We can't even see the garden." They walked up and down the fence searching for a way in, but it was high and had sharp iron spikes on top. "Darn, Darn, Darn," repeated Beryl. "I don't feel like coming all the way out here again. I wish the lord would welcome us today!"

"Can I help you?" came a voice from behind.

The girls turned around to see a priest, possibly a vicar, going by his white collar. He was bald with a well-trimmed white goatee beard, and he wore a white collar and a kindly smile. "Are you looking for something?" He made them feel immediately at ease.

"Hello, Father," Beryl perked up and flashed her 'charm' smile at the vicar. Carol was always amazed by how quickly Beryl could turn from bitter to sweet. "We wanted to take a look at the church gardens. We're doing a school project on old trees, and we were told there were some extra special ones in your church."

"That is most refreshing," the vicar smiled. "Lovely to have some visitors, and you are both welcome. My name is Paul. Please allow me to show you around."

He fished a bunch of keys out of his coat pocket and opened the gate. They followed him in. The gardens were well tended and pleasant, and the church had a welcoming feeling, the kind you might actually like to go to.

"The Church was built in 1789," he explained. "Now then, any particular trees you are interested in?" he asked.

"We like all sorts really," said Beryl. "But we are especially interested in large old ones that can grow hollow."

"Hollow trees, is it?" The vicar was amused. "Treasure-hunting, are we?" The girls glanced at each other with slight embarrassment. But the vicar didn't seem to mind. "No hollow trees here, but I can tell you a bit about them." They were turning the church corner and now stood by the graveyard. It was dotted with several old trees. "If you're looking for hollow trees, there is one main species you need to examine." He pointed to a large tree in the middle of the graveyard. "I mean the yew, of course."

Carol and Beryl stopped dead in their tracks, their minds instantly reaching the same conclusion. The yew, of course! Of course! How could they have been so dumb?

The vicar noticed their surprise. "Is that a revelation to you?"

The only revelation is how stupid we are, thought Carol, looking at Beryl who was rolling her eyes and thinking the same thing. OL_ _Y_ _ was part of the words 'Old Yew.'

CHAPTER 41

"Well, that's another piece of the riddle solved," said Beryl. "I can't believe I missed that!" They were on the long bike ride home.

Carol puffed while pedalling uphill. "It wasn't easy. But good progress. Now we have the second half to solve. I can think of two ways forward. One is to look up all the old hollow yew trees in the county, and the other is to look for a new church name."

"Sounds like a plan," said Beryl. "Library tomorrow."

"Library tomorrow." Carol smiled. "Our parents will be impressed."

* * *

The next day Mrs. Norman gave them a large pile of books about yew trees. Only the famous ones that had lived for thousands of years were listed. Some books claimed the yews were two or three thousand years old, others said five thousand. They saw pictures of giant hollow yews, some with houses built inside.

"I don't think our tree is one of the famous ones," said Carol. "If it was, someone would have found the treasure inside already. More likely it's just the beginning of a hollow. If that's the case, the tree won't be listed."

They turned their attention to church names. Both had already looked at all the 'Churches of C_R__' with R in the third place. But all they could come up with was Church of Christ. They scanned Church names in neighbouring counties but came up empty as well. By noon, they were frustrated and libraried out. They sat on the steps outside the building.

"I keep thinking we're missing a clue." Beryl was in crossword mode again.

"Bottom line, what are you saying?" Carol prodded her on the shoulder, having lost patience after the fruitless search.

"I'm saying two things, Nonco," said Beryl. "The first is that we are missing a letter, and the second is that it's time for ice cream."

"Now you're talking a language I understand," said Carol. "Onwards to the ice cream shop!"

Once the ice cream competition was concluded (pecan butter and snickers won), the girls continued their walk downtown. They loved walking on the cobbled high street, looking at the cute houses, the windows decorated with flower boxes, and brightly painted shops. But more 'For Sale' signs had popped up, and way too many Grockles were cruising the high street. Two of their favourite shops were closed, replaced by new souvenir shops, all selling the same rubbish.

"Our town is going to ruin," said Carol sadly. "If the textile factory closes after Christmas, that's it for most people. They might as well move our whole town to London next to the stock market."

There was nothing to say. Beryl was all too aware of the threat hanging over their heads. When the textile factory closed, it would be goodbye, Carol, goodbye friends, goodbye sweet town, and hello to empty houses and summer tourists. Their lives would be over. Even if they found money to keep Carol's house, they would be living in a ghost town.

Carol broke the sad spell. "My camping photos should be printed and ready in the shop. It's just around the corner, let's pick them up."

"Okay," said Beryl. "Nothing better to do."

As they approached the centre of town, they saw the Gang sitting on the iron railing by the traffic lights. That was where kids hung out when they had nothing better to do, and that was why the boys called themselves the High-Street Gang. They thought the name sounded threatening.

The girls had found out more about the boys from Jerry. Earnie, the plump leader of the gang, was actually called Ernst and was 'plain stupid.' Simon was 'a geek,' and Gimpy, who was half-French, was Alex, though his friends' nickname for him had stuck. Jerry had said Gimpy was 'just nasty,' and he had then offered to 'kick their butts' if the bullies gave the girls any more trouble. Carol had declined the offer, saying they could handle it themselves.

As soon as they saw the girls, the bullies launched into their banter.

"Ooh, Beryl and Peril! Don't think we won't get you. Just wait!"

"We're waiting." Beryl pulled a face and stuck her tongue out at them. "We'd love to teach you another lesson, seeing as you're too slow to learn. Fancy another mud bath, guys?"

The boys were so taken aback that Beryl dared answer that they were lost for words.

But just before they turned the corner, Gimpy shouted after them, "Get ready for a big surprise tomorrow afternoon. See you then! Your time has come." The boys laughed.

Beryl and Carol looked at each other with concern. What did he mean?

CHAPTER 42

The girls entered the old pharmacy, which still developed prints. It was beautifully arranged with dark wooden shelves with large drawers and big bottles full of white powders, some with weird labels like 'Nux Vomica' and 'Sulphur' on them.

"Good to see you are still open, Mr. Mundy!" Beryl was genuinely happy that he was.

"I'll be honest, girls, it's a struggle. So many of us have been swallowed by the giant chain stores or been bought for souvenir shops. Fortunately for me, even Londoners need pharmacies. We had a town meeting last night, and our last hopes are pinned on Princess Diana's visit in two months. She can make all the difference. When the Princess opens the new hospice, it will attract funds and doctors and health care workers and good business for pharmacies like mine, and for your mum's accounting firm, and for everyone else. It can save us. But if that doesn't happen, well, there'll be no jobs and our town will die." He handed Carol the prints. "That'll be £3.60, thanks."

Carol had to borrow £1.45 from Beryl. They were running low on funds; time to wash cars again.

They walked to the park and sat on their office bench.

"Let's have a look," said Beryl. Carol pulled the photos out of their bright yellow Kodak envelope.

The quality was excellent. Carol had a great camera, and she took her photography seriously. There were pictures of their tent, the campsite, Beryl on her bike and the first waterfalls. There was a self-portrait of both girls laughing, with the middle falls in the background, which Carol had taken using the camera's timer. There were close-ups of flowers and birds, one fantastic photo of a shiny blue and orange kingfisher diving into the river, which Carol had somehow caught with a high-speed shutter. Finally, there were some pictures of the map.

"I'd better hide these, so no one sees them accidentally." Carol tucked the map photos in the back of the envelope.

"Just a moment, Nonco," Beryl stuck her hand out. "Let's have a look at those."

Carol was tired and had had enough for the day. But she pulled the map pictures back out of the envelope and handed them to Beryl. Then she leant back on the bench and closed her eyes, soaking up the afternoon sun.

Beryl looked through the pictures and chose the best one. It was more focused and had better contrast than the others, and the light fell on it from a different angle. She looked at the drawing of the church with the cross. She looked at the large tree with the arrow pointing to its base. Nothing new. Then she looked at the writing. And there it was—something she had not seen before.

She stared at it for a long time before saying, "Listen up, Peril. It's not a C, it's an O!"

Carol had been dozing. Now she sat bolt upright and opened her eyes as if she had been bitten by a snake.

"What?" she said. "Say that again!"

"It's not a C. It's an O!" Beryl was excited. "Look here."

Carol held the photo so that the sunlight fell squarely on it. She peered at the first letter silently for a while.

Then she said in a half-whisper, "You know something, Nonco? You're right!"

Amazingly, the photo showed what they had not previously noticed. After the words 'The Church of' came the first letter 'C,' but they could now see that it was part of an 'O' with the last bit of the circle almost completely faded. Carol recollected something she had read in one of her photography books: 'A photo can see more than the naked eye. The camera shows everything.'

The girls' brains were revolving like windmills in a hurricane. This changed everything. The name was 'The Church of O_R...'

It took Beryl less than one minute to complete the puzzle.

"The Church of Our Lady," she said, and Carol nodded.

* * *

Fifteen minutes later, Beryl and Carol were back at the library.

"Back so soon, girls? I thought this was the summer holidays!"

a surprised Mrs. Norman greeted them.

"Horrible summer school projects," Beryl groaned. This had become the standard answer for everything, simply because it worked every time.

Beryl searched the books and Carol the internet, and soon they had a list of all the 'Churches of Our Lady' in their county. There were three in all—two to the east that were twenty-five miles and sixty miles away, and one to the west that was eighteen miles away.

They took out a map and located the Churches.

"Easy!" Carol was the first to solve it. "Mr. Phillips told us that the thief came from Ireland. Got to be the one to the west!"

The girls sat in the corner of the library, studying the map. Using her finger, Beryl traced a line westward from the caves to the Church of Our Lady. When she extended the line, it went straight through Snowdonia National Park to the Welsh coast, which was directly across the Irish Sea from Dublin.

"We know the thief or thieves came from Ireland." Beryl put forward her theory. "They are wanted by the police, so they avoid the ferry and take a small boat across the Irish sea to the West coast of Wales. Then they walk through the national park, which is an ideal place to hide, possibly hoping to get to England so they could sell whatever they had."

"That's how Tim worked it out!" Carol was full of admiration for Tim. "I saw another book on his library list which I haven't read yet, *Smuggling Stories of the British Isles*. I didn't realise it was important. Tim must have read about the treasure, realised the thief was being hunted and had to escape from Ireland in a hurry but avoid the Ferry. So, he researched smuggling routes over the Irish Sea to Wales and worked it out from there.

"The thief would have sailed across on a smugglers boat, then hiked through Snowdonia National Park until he reached the Church of Our Lady, where he hid the loot in the yew tree. Maybe it was too big or dangerous to carry. Then he walked through the forest for two or three days, avoiding the main roads. He was heading for the cave because it was a favourite place for thieves and smugglers to hide in. Maybe the boat people told him about the cave. He waited there for the heat to die down but never made it back for some reason. Perhaps he was sick or wounded."

"That all sounds very logical, but sadly there is a big flaw in your theory." Beryl looked at Carol with concern.

"What? What is it?" Carol was baffled.

"Who says it was a 'he,' Nonco?"

CHAPTER 43

The cycling was easy, and the twenty-one miles, which two weeks ago would have been a muscle-pulling ordeal, now seemed like a walk in the park. They stopped a couple of times to check the map and finally arrived at the tiny village where the Church of Our Lady was located. The church was marked on the map as being about a mile outside the village, which meant that they needed an ice cream stop. The girls parked their bikes by the small newspaper/post office/grocery/general goods store and went in.

There were no customers, and there wasn't much to buy anyway, only the usual magazines and chocolate bars, and an ice cream freezer. The girls chose two Cornettoes, mainly because there was not much choice. The shopkeeper was a middle-aged man wearing jeans and a worn green shirt, obviously bored stiff and eager for conversation. Beryl launched into her chat routine. After a few preliminaries concerning the weather and their bike journey, she asked about the Church of Our Lady.

"Oh, that old place," said the man, wiping the shop counter with an old rag. "Not a church anymore, I'm afraid. It was sold off to a Mr. Davis from London. He took a fancy to country life and our village and planned to renovate the church as a second home, but it never happened. 'Our Lady' was derelict since well before World War II, too far from the village centre. So, Mr. Davis got a bargain if you ask me. He only visits once a year, even less nowadays as he's getting old."

"So, is 'Our Lady' just standing empty?" Carol licked her Cornetto.

"Oh, no," the man replied. "A caretaker is looking after it, old Fred. Nasty chap, if you ask me. Been living there for near thirty years now. Mind you, he doesn't do much looking after the grounds, so it's just gone to ruin. Shame, if you ask me.

"Doesn't mix much, old Fred, never seen him drinking at the King's Head, and he only comes here if he has a parcel to collect. Goes shopping in town every Sunday at 10:00 AM, regular as clock-work. Shopping centres are the new churches. You would think he might support the local shops, but no, not old Fred, thinks he is too good for us, coming from London. So, he drives over an hour to the shopping centre instead of buying from me. It's because of people like him that our village is dying. I'm the last shop here, and I'm not sure how long I can last. When the post office closes, so does our village. Anyways, nothing for you to see at 'Our Lady,' if you ask me."

"That's a shame." Carol felt sorry to see the same thing happening here as in their town. "Actually, we were interested in the yew tree there. We've got this summer homework project to research a British tree, and we chose the yew. We heard there was a nice one there, so we came over to see it and take some pictures."

"Right you are, our yew used to be fairly well-known around these parts. It must be near a thousand years old, if you ask me, so it'll remember Robin Hood and the Magna Carta." The shopkeeper seemed proud to know this. "But now that it's on private property and Fred is in there, no one can visit it."

By the time he was done chatting, the girls had finished their Cornettoes. They thanked him and found a bench in the nearby park. It was a small, pretty park, but not well looked after. All the flowers were dead.

"Looks like another village moving to London," Carol said sadly.

"Useful intel, but good or bad?" Beryl wanted to move on.

"Both." Carol gave this some thought. "Good, because the church has been closed since before the war, so it's unlikely anyone found the treasure. But bad because we can't get in."

"Yep, old Fred doesn't sound like the welcoming sort, if you ask me." Beryl mimicked the shopkeeper. "Still, we have to have a look."

They checked their map. The road was a dead end, leading to nowhere other than the church and vast forest all around. No wonder people stopped going—two miles was too far a walk on a Sunday. The girls got their bikes and set off for what they hoped would be the last leg of their long journey. The road was rough and unpaved.

As soon as they arrived and saw the church, their hearts skipped a beat. There was no doubt that this was the place! The church looked exactly like the drawing on the map—a classic church building with a big cross on the front of the roof, the long window, and a vast old yew tree in exactly the right spot.

The two girls stood on the other side of the road staring at the building with astonishment.

"This is it," whispered Carol. "We're here. We made it! Unbelievable."

Beryl also had an 'unbelievable' look on her face.

"Yep, this is it all right, we made it!" Then she thought for a while and said, "I'm getting this strange feeling—like we are so close and yet so far. But here we are, so let's get that treasure."

"If it's still there," said Carol. But she stood up with a determined look on her face. "It has to be there. If someone already found the treasure, we would have heard or read about it, or the shopkeeper would have told us. Come on, we've worked hard for this, and it's ours. Let's do it."

CHAPTER 44

The church was surrounded by forest. Probably the forest the thief had walked through. The girls could imagine him leaving the ferry, then travelling through back roads and forests, until finally stumbling on the remote church. He would have decided it was safer to hide the treasure and lay low until the commotion died down and the search had stopped. After hiding the treasure in the yew, he probably carried on through the forest until he reached the falls and the caves. For some reason, the thief never made it back to pick up the treasure; otherwise, he wouldn't have bothered to draw the map. Perhaps he was wounded or sick or had a fight with other robbers hiding in the cave, or someone stopped him returning. Maybe the goods were just too hot to sell for many years, and he was anxious he would forget where the treasure was, or he was leaving the map for an accomplice. The girls had no way of knowing.

The Church had a sinister, ghostly look and felt dark and scary. It looked like something from a vampire story and sent a chill down their spines. The yard was surrounded by a wire fence on top of an old stone wall. There was a gate with a padlock and a faded sign saying, 'Private property, keep out!' The garden was unkempt and wild. Weeds covered the paths and old flower beds; the trees had not been pruned and were sprouting thick and bushy in every direction.

But, in the middle of the churchyard stood the magnificent

old yew, with a massive girth. They stood by the fence, admiring the tree and imagining all the births, marriages, christenings, and deaths it had witnessed over the centuries. A year would seem like a day to it, and a day like a minute. How much wisdom would have been absorbed into its roots? The girls peered over the fence to see if it was hollow, but they couldn't get a good view.

They went to the gate. There was no bell or buzzer, which was not a welcoming sign.

"What next?" Carol asked. "No way in."

"Next, we sweet talk Fred," said Beryl. She cupped her hands to her mouth and shouted, "Hello, anyone home?"

The door opened, and an old man with a walking stick came out. He was wearing a well-worn brown tweed jacket and slippers.

He walked towards the gate, looking very unhappy about being disturbed.

Beryl launched her best charm offensive.

"Good morning, sir!" She said in her polite little girl voice, combined with her best tucking hair behind the ear routine, which had never failed yet. " | Lovely day, isn't it? Thanks soooo much for coming out to see us. How are you today, sir? And what a lovely house you have."

Beryl's charm offensive hit the wall like a speeding car without a driver.

"Who are you, and what the heck are you disturbing me for?" growled the man in a thick South London accent.

Beryl was surprised. No one had ever resisted her charm attack before. She launched an improved version.

"So sorry to disturb you, sir," she said in her little girl voice, now using the helpless version which was a sure winner. "We were just really interested in your church. You see, sir, we have this school project and..."

Bang. The charm offence was shot out of the sky and spun out of control.

"Stop right there. This isn't a church anymore, as you can see. It's a private home." He pointed at the sign.

"I understand, sir, of course it is, sir. But we thought that perhaps we could..."

"Well, you thought wrong!" Fred raised his stick in a threatening way. "Maybe you didn't understand the first time, so I'll say it one last time before you turn around and leave. This place is no longer a church. It's a private home, and it belongs to Mr. Davis from London. I just look after it. If you want to come in or to know anything, you have to talk to Mr. Davis. Maybe you can find his name in the phone book. Until then, never show your faces here again. Goodbye."

The shocked Beryl was about to open her mouth again, but Carol caught her by the sleeve and gently pulled her back.

"Don't waste your time, Maria," she said. "Let's get out of here."

They crossed the road and got on their bikes, the man looking after them to make sure they left.

If there was a dead-end competition, this one would win the gold medal.

The girls rode their bikes back to town saying nothing. They were shaken from the bad experience with Fred, so they went to chill in the park.

"Perhaps we can phone Mr. Davis in London," Carol said when they arrived in town.

"Right, let's just look him up in the phone book. There are probably only a hundred thousand Davises in London."

"So, what's next?" Carol asked, though she knew very well.

"Well, if you ask me, Dame Peril," Beryl was still in shopkeeper talk, "come this Sunday, you and I will be shopping at the church while Fred goes praying at the shopping centre."

Carol nodded reluctantly. The thought gave her goosebumps.

"Let's go home. Remember we have to avoid the Gang today."

When they arrived at their homes, what they saw made them both sick to the stomach. Carol's face turned red and then blue. Beryl felt as though she were trapped in the cave again, about to be sick.

Carol's parents were standing in the garden with another family. By the way that Carol's father was pointing, it was clear that he was selling the house to the visitors. The other family was a father, mother, and two kids. One was a little girl, and the other was Gimpy.

When Gimpy saw Beryl and Carol standing speechless by the gate, he waved cheerfully and gloated in his most sarcastic tone,

"Hello. We've come to buy your house, Peril. My friends and I will be seeing a lot more of you, Beryl."

* * *

The girls sat behind Mrs. E's house. Beryl was trembling. She imagined walking to school in the morning with Gimpy right next to her, maybe with his two stupid friends. There would be no one to talk to or help her to fight back. She would have no access to the river. Even the Meukki would not be fun alone. She would have to hide in her room, with Sam pestering her. She might as well die.

"You moving out is bad enough but leaving me with that pig living next door is too much. I would rather move to Birmingham with you," she groaned.

Carol had spoken to her mother.

"Gimpy's family wants a place by the river. First, they tried to buy Mrs. E's house, but the London people got to it first, so they are making sure that doesn't happen again. My dad told me that houses by the river are a great investment if you have the cash to spare. Gimpy's family wants to move in early next year. His father owns a big pharmaceutical company in France, so they are loaded."

"Ugh, big pharma." Beryl was in tears.

But there was worse news. Carol felt sick when she spoke about it.

"My mother says Gimpy's family are offering us more money than we ever hoped for, which means my dad can come and live with us when we move. Otherwise, he has to stay in Cambridge."

The awful choice was between splitting Carol's family apart or Gimpy living next door. Beryl's mind went numb.

The girls were silent for a long while. Finally, Carol threw a stone in the water and stood up. "This is not going to happen. We have to find the treasure. Maybe it's worth a huge amount, even ten thousand pounds, and we can use it to convince my parents not to sell or at least to keep my dad with us."

Beryl dried her eyes.

"I can't imagine any treasure being worth that much. But we have to try."

CHAPTER 45

It was 9:59 AM on Sunday morning, and the girls were hiding behind a clump of trees opposite the Church of Our Lady. Their bikes were concealed nearby, ready for a hasty getaway. They were carrying rucksacks with digging forks and trowels along with snacks, water, and torches.

Exactly one minute later, the door opened, and Fred came out. The girls retreated behind the trees. They heard the creak of the big gate opening, then Fred starting his car, driving out of the gate, getting out again to lock the gate behind him, and finally driving off. They waited for another minute to make sure, then came out of hiding.

"Let's go, Dame Peril." Beryl pointed to the yew. "End game, I hope! We have two-or-three-hours tops."

They walked around the fence until they found a place where the wire was sagging. They had never broken into someone's garden before, and they weren't too keen on the idea, especially not into Fred's garden. Beryl's mouth was dry, and Carol could feel her knees trembling, but they had to do this. Beryl stood on the old stone wall, put a leg over the sagging wire fence and climbed over. Carol followed.

"Let's have a look through the window," Beryl said.

"What for? We need to get going. There's no time." But Beryl was already by the window, so Carol joined her.

What they saw was worse than any vampire. Their blood ran cold.

They were looking into the kitchen. In the centre of the room was a large kitchen table, and on it, arranged in tidy piles, were six rows of sealed plastic bags filled with white powder. Next to the piles stood a set of high-quality scales.

Carol yanked Carol back. "Drugs! No wonder Fred doesn't want anyone around. This is the perfect place, no one ever comes here. That's why he goes to town every Sunday rather than shopping in the village. Maybe he's selling the drugs."

Beryl was shaking, her face as white as the powder in the bags.

"Carol, if he catches us, he won't just beat us up. He will kill us! Let's get out of here! This is really dangerous."

"No way. We've come this far. We're not giving up now. Let's work fast. But we can't let him catch us, or we really will be dead."

They raced through the jungle of weeds to the old yew tree. It was situated in the middle of the church's spooky graveyard, which gave them the shivers even though it was broad daylight. Carol thought she could feel the ghosts, and Beryl imagined red-eyed vampires hiding behind the gravestones.

They circled the tree, looking for a hollow spot. There was none! The girls felt a sense of panic rise within them. Could this be a mistake? Was it the wrong yew after all? They walked around again, but the trunk appeared solid.

"What? How? No hollow. Where is it?" Beryl mumbled.

"Hang on," said Carol, "let's check properly. Look low." They crawled around the base, looking close to the roots, and there it was. On the opposite side to the Church was the smallest of holes at the base of the trunk.

Beryl lay down and shone her torch into the opening. She could just see a wider cavern beyond. There was a large, dark and empty space inside the tree.

"This is it!" she said confidently, wiping the dirt from her pants. "Either the earth covered the opening over the years, or the thief covered up after himself. I can see why this was the perfect spot to hide something. If you didn't know the tree was hollow, you might easily miss it."

"Okay, great," said Carol. "We better start digging fast." She looked at her watch. "It's 10:20. Two and a half hours left at most."

They pulled out the gardening tools and got to work, taking turns to dig around the small opening. The earth was hard, which made progress slow, and before long, they were panting, sweating, and dirty. But after half an hour, they had created a definite opening leading into the hollow.

"Three-minute break, then carry on," said Carol, pulling some snacks out of the bag.

"What do we do if Fred comes back?" Beryl worried.

Carol thought for a moment, munching her bar.

"We sneak out, run to the fence, then leg it to the bikes. If he follows us, we ride into the forest. He won't be able to go in there with his car, and he has a walking stick, so he can't run. But one more thing. If he catches one of us, the other has to get away and call the police. He won't dare kill one and leave the other as a witness. But if he catches us both, there is no doubt he will kill us. If he gets me, you get to the village and call the cops. Promise?"

Beryl thought, then nodded.

"Promise. And you promise, too."

Carol nodded. The friends did a quick handshake, then got back to work, taking turns digging around the hole. Twenty minutes later, the opening was big enough for Beryl to crawl in. She was anxious about being in another small space, but she said nothing. Carol watched her wriggle into the hollow and remembered how her thin, tall friend had managed to enter the cave behind the falls. Handy thin Finns! She waited for a moment and saw the light from

Beryl's torch shining through the entrance hole.

"What can you see?" Carol demanded impatiently.

"Oh, there's a cinema complex and a magic rabbit hutch in here," Beryl said in a serious tone.

"I'll kill you, Nonco. Come on! What's in there?"

"Big hollow space, pretty amazing. After the cave, this is like the Albert Hall. Quite a few beetles. No treasure yet. But the hollow might be bigger under the earth, we'll have to dig. I'm starting. Work on the entrance till you can get through."

Carol dug around the entrance with renewed enthusiasm. Five minutes later, she was in with Beryl. Beryl shone the torch around for Carol to see.

The tree was as incredible inside as out. Carol could see the veins, arteries and muscles of the tree, if you could call them that, all covered by a thin layer of green moss. It was the size of a cupboard, and both girls could barely fit inside. The air was dank and chilly. Beryl pointed her torch to the floor below. It was apparent that the hollow continued underneath the ground, and Beryl had already started digging.

Carol peeked at her watch. It was quarter past eleven, which meant that Fred would be back sometime within the next hour or so.

"Got to keep going fast." Beryl read her mind. "I'll dig, and you clear the earth out of the opening. Let's take turns."

Space was tight, the earth was hard, and they had to shine a torch to see what they were doing. Beryl dug furiously, and Carol pushed the dirt out. Ten minutes later, they changed places. Beryl had dug a 30cm deep hole in the middle. "Nothing here, widen it out a bit," she said, passing Carol the trowel. "I might have missed it if it's not in the middle." She began pushing earth out of the hole.

The girls were breathing heavily and sweating buckets, although the air inside the tree was cool, all the time conscious of the minutes ticking by, but they found nothing. This was a race against time, but even as they dug furiously, the same thoughts were going through their heads, urging them to just walk away. Could this be a wild fantasy? Maybe it was all a hoax? Perhaps someone just drew the map for fun and was messing with their heads. Maybe Tim never existed, or they were in the wrong church, or the treasure was just a cheap trinket. There were so many things that could go wrong. Beryl started to say, "Maybe we spent the whole summer on some wild goo—"

Clang.

Carol's trowel hit metal. To be exact, it was more of a small 'ting' than a clang, but the effect was as if a church bell had just rung inside the tree. Both girls sat bolt upright. Beryl gasped, and Carol hit her head on the inside of the trunk but didn't even notice. They had hit metal!

That was the very same moment they heard Fred's car at the gate. It was as if they were defrosted and instantly frozen again. Their bodies were paralysed, but their hearts were beating like two gazelles being chased by a pack of hyenas. They held their breath both from the excitement of finding something and the fear of Fred catching them inside the tree and beating the living daylight out of them with his stick.

Beryl moved first. She could hear Fred opening the gate and then getting back in his car. This was the moment to act, while the car engine drowned out any noise. She wriggled out of the opening and pulled the two rucksacks into the hollow. Then she gathered any earth that had spread sideways to directly behind the tree so it could not be seen from the church. A moment later she was back inside the tree, just as Fred turned the engine off. They heard the car door opening and banging shut. The girls sat without batting an eyelid, praying that Fred's face would not appear in the opening.

They listened to Fred crunching the gravel as he walked from the car back and forth to the church, probably bringing in the shopping. Finally, they heard the slamming of the car door, followed by the church's side door closing.

They sat quietly for a few moments to give Fred time to settle down, then Carol shone her torch at the spot she had been digging, using her other hand to clear some earth away. Beryl crouched forward and looked. There it was, clearly visible at the bottom of the hole they had dug—a grey metal object, perhaps tin or iron. Beryl felt it with her hand, then looked up at Carol and gave the thumbs up and a silent fist bump. The girls were so excited they almost forgot about Fred.

Using their hands so as not to make a noise, they cleared the soil from around the metal. It was now clear that it was a metal box with a handle on top. The box was still stuck fast in the ground, so they dug around it. Their fingers and nails hurt, but they didn't notice because of the adrenaline pumping through their veins. Beryl held the handle and pulled slowly and gently. The box moved out of the earth on one side. She gave it a wiggle, and then it was in her hand. She held it up, and Carol shone the torch at it. It was a square tin box, the size of a book, with a hinged handle on top. On the front was a clasp that was locked shut with an ancient, rusty padlock that would need one of those big old keys to open it. Beryl felt the weight of the box in her hand. She gave it a light shake. Something moved inside!

The girls looked at each other, excited and exhausted at the same time. They would have both danced for joy if there was room to move in the tree, and if they weren't terrified of Fred hearing them, so instead they gave a silent high five and Carol mouthed, "We did it!" Beryl handed her the box, and she held it in both hands and gave it a little shake. There was something inside.

They rested for a moment until they got their breath back. Carol shone the torch at her hands—they were blistered and bleeding. Nothing she could do about that; it was time to go. Beryl packed the tools and torches into her rucksack, and Carol placed the box inside hers.

Before they left, Carol whispered in Beryl's ear, "Run like your life depends on it and remember, if he gets me, *don't stop*. Get to the village and phone the cops."

Beryl nodded.

The girls crawled out of the hole, and for a moment they were blinded by the light. Their bodies were stiff and aching so they could hardly stand straight. They stretched and got ready to bail. As quietly as they could, the girls crept around the tree. And there, standing outside the church and looking straight at them, stood Fred, with a big stick in his hand.

CHAPTER 46

F red and the girls stood looking at each other, all blinking with surprise.

Fred came to his senses first.

"You are trespassing and stealing," he said in a threatening voice. "I don't know what you have seen or stolen, but I aim to find out. And because you're on my property, I have the right to hit you in self-defence, even kill you if I feel in danger," he sneered, lifting his stick.

Beryl knew she could easily escape because she was younger and faster than Fred and played basketball. Avoiding people at speed was second nature to her. But Carol, what about Carol? She couldn't leave her friend to deal with Fred alone.

She turned to Carol.

"Go, Judith, go! I'll distract him, I'll be alright. You have the box, and we can't lose that. As soon as I give the signal, run for the fence!"

Carol hesitated, but Fred was already beginning to move towards them, his stick held high.

Instead of running to the fence, Beryl ran to the front gate, trying to distract Fred from Carol. It worked. He followed her, moving surprisingly fast for someone with a walking stick. When he was halfway to her, Beryl screamed, "Run, Judith, run!" Carol took the cue and ran directly past the confused Fred to the wall. She was at the fence before he could even change direction. She stuck her foot on top of the stone wall, and in a moment, she was over.

Fred realised he had lost one child, so he focused on Beryl. He ran to the gate, again moving remarkably quickly. It was clear Fred had been in situations like this before. He held the stick high in one arm, with the other arm spread out wide, moving forward in a zig-zag motion to confuse Beryl.

Beryl used one of the basketball cuts she had learned from Jerry. She feigned a turn towards the fence, the direction he expected her to go, and when he moved that way, she suddenly turned back towards the tree. Beryl could easily run a ring around him, even around the church if she needed to. But she forgot one thing. This was not a basketball court; it was a loose gravel driveway. Her fast change of direction caused her to slide on the small stones, and she fell to the ground, twisting her ankle. She felt a sharp pain. She would not be able to run.

"Got you now, thief," he mocked in his south London accent. "Say 'Hello' to my stick!" He raised it high in the air as he advanced on Beryl slowly and menacingly.

Beryl knew she was a goner. He might not kill her, because Carol had escaped, but he could do some severe damage with that stick, and Fred looked as if breaking one or two of her bones would give him nothing but pleasure. She closed her eyes and curled up in a tight ball to protect her face and stomach, bracing herself for the blows. Fred moved forward.

Just as Beryl was expecting the first strike, she heard an ear-piercing scream, followed by a yelp of pain. Beryl opened her eyes and saw Carol hanging on to Fred from behind, her left arm tight around his neck and her right arm clutching the end of his stick. At the same time, she was sinking her teeth deep into his shoulder. She began shaking her head like a terrier holding a rabbit, and Fred was screaming in pain. He dropped the stick and tried to knock Carol off him, but she stayed behind so he could not reach her, all the time biting deeper and shaking her head for maximum effect. Fred screamed again and tried to beat Carol off, slapping at her head from behind. Suddenly, without warning, Carol let go and gave Fred a tremendous kick in the back of his bad knee, which caused it to buckle. Fred fell on the ground, clutching his shoulder.

Now that her mouth was free, Carol shouted, "Run, Maria, run!"

Beryl was already hobbling toward the fence. Carol ran after her, gave her a shoulder to lean on, then a leg up over the wall. When Beryl was over Carol stuck her leg on the stone wall, just as she heard Fred running on the gravel and screaming.

"I'm going to kill you!"

Carol felt the stick crash into her thigh just as she rolled over the fence. It hurt like hell!

The girls limped to their bikes and pulled them out of the forest. Carol picked up the rucksack she had thrown over the fence before running back for Beryl. Just as they were about to mount the bikes and cycle off, they heard Fred's car starting up. They looked at each other in horror.

"Get going, now!" Beryl shouted as she jumped on the bike. "Peddle like the devil."

The girls raced down the road as fast as their injured, aching bodies allowed. They knew that Fred would have to unlock the gate, which would take a moment, but he wouldn't be so stupid as to get out of the car to lock the gate behind him.

"Take the first path you see into the forest," Carol yelled.

They rode like crazy for about two minutes. They could now hear Fred's car moving in the distance behind them. He must have opened the gate.

"There!" shouted Beryl.

Carol saw it—a small path leading into the forest on her right.

Beryl swerved and jumped the ditch with her bike, and Carol was straight after her. A moment later, they were riding the bumpy forest path, jumping up and down on roots, sticks, and stones. Their bikes could handle it, but their aching bodies found it painful. After a minute, they swerved between the trees and threw the bikes on the ground. They could hear Fred's car racing down the road, so they dived on the hard forest floor, lying still and not daring to move an inch. A moment later, they saw the red flash of his car between the trees as it sped by. Beryl signalled to Carol not to move. It was best they stayed there until he gave up and drove back.

It took 20 minutes. Fred must have driven to the village and looked around, then driven up and down the road a few times. They heard his car approaching, this time much slower. They could imagine Fred was in physical and mental pain, both from Carol's bite and from knowing the girls had been in his yard and had probably seen the drugs. He might find the hollow in the yew before too long, but that would not help him much anymore.

The girls heard Fred's engine come to a stop at the church. They waited silently for another ten minutes. Carol's leg was throbbing and swollen, and Beryl's ankle was hurting badly. They limped back towards the road, pushing their bikes, and peeked from behind the trees. Fred was running back and forth, hurriedly throwing the white plastic bags into his car. He was trying to get away! The two girls jumped on their bikes and cycled down the road towards the village, going as fast as their aching bodies allowed.

When they got to the village, they stopped by a red phone booth. Beryl made the 999 call. They had to get Fred arrested before he came looking for them. Beryl spoke for one minute, then came out of the booth and gave Carol a thumbs up.

Then she hit her hard on the head with her rucksack. Twice.

"Ow!!" Carol yelped.

"That's for breaking your promise!" Beryl hit her again. Then she gave her a huge hug and kissed Carol's face all over. Both girls were crying. But there was no time to waste.

"Let's move, now! He could come at any moment."

The girls jumped on their bikes and raced out of the village towards home. Two minutes later they heard the sirens, followed by two police cars speeding towards the village. They just kept going, two small girls on a Sunday bike ride.

* * *

By the time they reached the outskirts of their town, they were aching bundles of agony. They stopped at the side of the road, catching their breath.

"We can't go into town with this," Beryl pointed at the treasure bag. "We have to hide it."

Carol nodded, still panting from the ride.

"Meukki," is all she managed to say.

Beryl knew she was right. It was too dangerous to ride through town, in case someone stopped them, or anything happened that could jeopardise the treasure. Bringing it home was tricky. Their own little house was the safest option. They turned off the main road and cycled around town, using the old dust road that led to the forest from the other direction. They rode till the edge of the forest and stopped. No one ever used this road, so they had a moment to rest and reflect.

"Remember how this all started?" Carol looked around. This was the exact place where they had been cornered by the High-Street Gang.

"Just thinking the same thing," Beryl replied.

It had only been five months since they had escaped down this road following an old tin can. So much had happened since then that it seemed like five years. They had escaped the bullies, found the clearing, built the Kon-Taki and their beautiful house, found Tim's box and letter, followed clues to the waterfall, crawled in caves, fought off Hank, deciphered the map and found the yew and treasure, and finally escaped nasty Fred. And now, like salmon swimming upriver to the place of their birth, the girls had gone full circle to the point where it had all started, the only difference being that, instead of an old tin can, they had a box with a real treasure inside it—or not. And just for this moment, it didn't matter, because, while their previous lives had felt like an empty tin can, they were now fulfilled by a treasure far more valuable than any object—the treasure of having a sense of purpose, determination, and courage to do what was needed in every situation.

"How did all of this ever happen?" Beryl thought aloud.

"I guess we dared to follow an empty can into the unknown," Carol replied.

They got back on their bikes and rode into the forest.

CHAPTER 47

Before this, they had only ever walked through the forest to their Meukki. Even though the girls were exhausted and in severe pain, it took less than ten minutes to reach the point where they had first heard the river and found their clearing.

"Wow," said Beryl. "That was fast!"

"Me like," smiled Carol, using her Gorilla voice.

They laid down their bikes and walked the rest of the way to the clearing—and there it was, their own sweet home in the most beautiful spot in the world. The pains, aches, tension, and fears of the day melted away, and they felt at peace. They sat down on the porch, enjoying the afternoon sunshine and the sounds of nature. Beryl dished out the Arnica from her remedy kit, Carol got some biscuits, and they munched away.

When they were finished, Beryl stood up stretching her aching body and said, "Let's show Tim."

They walked over to Tim's shrine. Rosa was sprouting her first buds. Carol took the box out of her rucksack.

"Here you go, Tim," she said. "Your treasure, our treasure, we found it! And we worked out how you discovered it, you clever man. And yes, we do remember you deserve a cut. Sorry, we can't open it yet because it's locked."

They sat silently, trying to listen to Tim's answer, imagining that he wore a big 'told-you-so' grin on his face. They stayed for a while, then Carol looked at her watch. It was 4:15 PM. "We better get going," she said.

Things were not good at home. Both Beryl and Carol's parents were moody, probably for the same reason. Of course, it was good news that Carol's parents got an excellent price for their house, which would make the money situation much more manageable, but they hated the idea of leaving their lovely cottage and their best friends. And Beryl's parents hated the idea of rich snobs moving next door. Bang goes the neighbourhood.

"When will we have to leave, Mum?" Carol was in despair.

"We told them not till after February or March. Who knows, maybe my firm will get the hospice account. The good news is that we get one last Christmas here with Beryl's family."

* * *

Beryl and Carol met the next morning, relieved to escape the dark atmosphere at home.

"I hope that stupid treasure is worth something. Probably a painting that rotted inside the box." Beryl was in a mood.

Carol was unhappy too, but she wanted to find out what was in the box as soon as possible.

"Let's go buy a hacksaw. I could learn to pick the lock but that would need special tools, so it'll be easier to cut it."

The girls walked over to the hardware store. Written in golden faded letters on the glass front were the words 'Home and Hardware Association.' It was one of the few real stores remaining in town, probably because the owner was headstrong and refused to give in to bullying chain stores and tourist shops that tried to kick him out. Old Mr. Sherman stood at the counter, wearing the same worn blue shirt he always wore.

When Carol asked for a hacksaw, he asked, "Lots of different hacksaws here. What's it for?"

"Cutting an old lock," Carol stuck to the truth.

"You'll need a blowtorch as well. Otherwise, the saw will just slide off the metal." He handed Carol both items and showed her how to use the portable blowtorch.

Beryl used all the money they had left from washing the cars. They were broke again.

The girls walked through the forest, lost in thought about what lay ahead. Either it would turn out to be nothing, or it would help them save Carol's house, or at least stop Gimpy moving in. They had been looking forward to this moment with excitement and anxiety for so long, and today was the big day.

Carol suggested making tea and resting for a bit, but Beryl was having none of that.

"Now or never, trick or treat, make or break, shine or rust, gold or dust. Let's do it."

Carol got the blowtorch and hacksaw, and Beryl went to fetch the box from under the bushes.

A moment later, she shouted to Carol, "It's not here!"

"What?!" Carol gasped.

"I know I put it here, but it's vanished!" Beryl was looking around the bushes frantically and rubbing her head.

"No way!" Carol was alarmed.

"Just kidding, Nonco," Beryl laughed, showing her the box.

"I'll kill you!" Carol threw a pinecone, just missing Beryl's head. "You nearly gave me a heart attack." But she laughed. Beryl's little trick broke the tension.

Beryl placed the box on top of a flat stone. Carol lit the blowtorch, and a hot red flame burst from the nozzle. She turned the knob on the side until the fire became pointed and blue. She aimed the hissing flame at the old lock's shackle. After a few minutes, the metal began to change colour, shining in silver, red, green and blue.

She turned off the blowtorch, and they waited. Once the lock cooled, Carol held the box and the lock, and Beryl began sawing. It took a minute or two for the saw to catch, but then the blade dug in, just as Mr. Sherman had promised.

Three minutes later, the shackle was cut. Carefully, Carol removed the lock. The box was ready to open.

Beryl took a deep breath and pulled the hinged latch open. It was stiff, but it came. She tried to open the box, but it was tightly sealed with rust. Carol went to the house and got a screwdriver, and Beryl prized the lid from all sides until it loosened. It reminded her of Tim's tobacco tin. She looked at Carol, and they nodded at each other. This was the big moment.

Beryl opened the lid.

Inside was an old brown leather pouch tied with a drawstring. Beryl picked it up and held it carefully, weighing it in her hand. There was something inside, and it felt substantial. She pulled the string, and the bow knot opened. Beryl put her hand in and pulled out something wrapped in wax paper. It was quite large and heavy. She placed it on the flat stone and unwrapped the parcel.

And there it was.

Beryl and Carol said nothing—all they could do was stare. They were gobsmacked. Time stood still and then vanished. Once or twice, they tried to speak but were unable to. The kingfisher flew close by, splendid in shiny blue and orange, but they didn't notice. They just sat wide-eyed and gawked.

After about three-quarters of an eternity, Carol managed to produce a sound.

"I can't believe it," she whispered.

"What?" Beryl mumbled out of a dream.

"I know what this is," Carol said slowly. "Congratulations, Your Majesty."

CHAPTER 48

In front of them was the most beautiful object they had ever seen or were ever likely to see. It was a piece of jewellery, but nothing like a regular piece of jewellery. The jewel was the size of a tea saucer, and it glittered, shone, sparkled, gleamed, and dazzled with hundreds of shiny diamonds arranged in the shape of a star. In the middle was a three-leafed clover made of green emeralds, and behind that, a cross of deep, red rubies. Around the cross were the letters *Quis Separabit* and some Roman numerals. The girls had never imagined anything like this existed. It was spectacular.

They stared for a while longer. Carol said something, but it just bounced off Beryl, who was still too dumbfounded to talk.

"It's the Grand Master Star," Carol repeated.

"What?" repeated Beryl, one more time.

"I think you need a cup of tea," said Carol.

Beryl nodded. She did need a cup of tea. Carefully, Carol wrapped the Star in the wax paper and put it back in the leather pouch and placed it in the box—it was too dazzling to look at for a long time. Then she led the stunned Beryl back to the house.

Silently, she boiled some water on the camp stove. It was still too difficult to say anything. Every time they were about to mutter a sentence, a hundred other thoughts bumped it out of the way. Carol made tea in the pot the proper way: warm the pot, one teaspoon for her, one for Beryl, and one for the pot, pour the water, one stir, cover with a towel, and let it brew for five minutes. Warm the cup with hot water, milk first, and pour the tea very slowly when ready. That made the perfect cup, and making it slowly helped to calm the mind. They sat at the table and sipped their tea with the box sitting on their table between them. The warm drink calmed their minds.

"What is that thing?" Beryl finally managed to speak. "It's out of this world!"

"It's the Grand Master Star," Carol explained, "and it belongs to the royal family. I read a little about it in Tim's lost treasures book, but I never imagined... so I didn't read the whole chapter. Ireland... Dublin... of course! Unbelievable!"

Carol walked over to the bookshelf and pulled out *The Lost and Stolen Treasures of England for Young Readers* which she had borrowed from the library. She leafed through the book until she found the page. There was a black and white picture, which she showed to Beryl.

DUBLIN METROPOLITAN POLICE.

DETECTIVE DEPARTMENT,
EXCHANGE COURT,
DUBLIN, 8th July, 1907.

STOLEN

From a Safe in the Office of Arms, Dublin Castle, during the past month, supposed by means of a false key.

GRAND MASTER'S DIAMOND STAR.

A Diamond Star of the Grand Master of the Order of St. Patrick composed of brilliants (Brazilian stones) of the purest water, 4½ by 4¼ inches, consisting of eight points, four greater and four lesser, issuing from a centre enclosing a cross of rubies and a trefoil of emeralds surrounding a sky blue enamel circle with words, "Quis Separabit MDCCLXXXIII." in rose diamonds engraved on back. Value about £14,000.

Beryl looked at the picture and read the description. She mulled over it for a long time, looking dumbfounded.

"Carol. This is it. We found it! After 90 years," she finally managed to say.

Carol nodded and pointed at the date on the poster.

"90 years, one month, and ten days, to be exact."

"And look!" Beryl was excited. "It says it is worth 14,000 pounds! Do you realise that with inflation over all that time it could be worth as much as 20,000 pounds? That would be enough to keep your house!"

Carol was excited. Of course! Inflation. 20,000 pounds! The Star could save the day.

"Tell me the story," said Beryl, leaning back in her chair and closing her eyes.

Carol cleared her throat and began reading.

"The Mysterious Case of the Missing Irish Crown Jewels:

"*The Irish Crown Jewels were the Star and Badge of the Order of St Patrick. The Order of St. Patrick was a British Order of knights established in 1783 by King George the III. It was associated with Ireland, and its purpose was to honour Irish celebrities and friends of the empire. The British monarch was Sovereign of the Order, and the Lord Lieutenant of Ireland was the Grand Master. The Jewels were made from diamonds belonging to Queen Charlotte. They were presented to the Order by King William the IV in 1831. They were to be worn by the monarch or by the Grand Master on ceremonial occasions.*

"*The two pieces were magnificent works of craftsmanship. The Grand Master Star was a large pendant that consisted of 400 Brazilian white diamonds arranged in an eight-pointed star. In the middle were a shamrock of emeralds and a cross of rubies. The second piece was an oval badge composed of an emerald shamrock and a ruby cross surrounded by Brazilian diamonds. Both gems had the motto of the order—'Quis Separabit?' MDCCLXXIII (1783), meaning 'Who can separate us?' —written in rose diamonds.*

"*The jewels were kept in a special safe in Dublin Castle under the custody of the Ulster King of Arms who, at the time of the theft, was Sir Arthur Vicars.*

"*In 1903, a new strongroom was built especially for the safe containing the jewels. However, once it was finished, the builders realised that they had forgotten to measure the safe and found that it was too big to fit through the door. Oops! They decided to leave the safe in the library until they got a smaller one, but as these things go, they never did.*

"*Never mind, they thought. The jewels were well-guarded by the Ulster King of Arm's staff, and by a patrol of policemen and soldiers. Just down the road was the Dublin detective's headquarters. It all seemed secure enough.*

"*But the weak link was Sir Vicars, who was quite relaxed about security, so much so that he frequently lent the keys to his friends and junior officers. One night, after a drunken party, he woke up to find the jewels around his neck.*

"*On the morning of July the 6th, 1907, the cleaner found the door of the safe wide open. He informed Sir Vicars immediately, who casually replied, 'Is that so?' and took no further action. Later that day, Vicars gave one of his messengers the key and asked him to deposit some valuables in the safe. The messenger found the safe door unlocked and immediately informed Vicars. He finally came to inspect and discovered that the Crown Jewels had vanished. It was almost a month since they had last been seen.*

"*The timing could not have been worse. Four days later, King Edward VII and Queen Alexandra were due to visit the Irish International Exhibition. When the King heard of the theft, he flew into a rage. The robbery was considered an insult to the King and a huge embarrassment to the Irish government.*

"A massive investigation was launched, and there were many suspects and theories. The police found that the lock had not been tampered with but had been opened with a key. It looked like an inside job, and the main suspect was Vicars, as he was the only person in possession of the safe keys. Vicars denied guilt for the rest of his life. There was no proof, and so Vicars was charged with negligence and was fired along with his staff. Initially, Vicars refused to resign his position, and when he finally did, he would not hand over the keys!

"Other officers were investigated, including Francis Shackleton, brother of the famous explorer Ernest Shackleton. Strangely, most of the suspects met with untimely and highly suspicious deaths. One died in a shooting accident, another in a motor car accident, and Sir Vicars himself was assassinated. Shackleton was declared bankrupt and was imprisoned for fraud.

"There were many investigations and rumours over the years, but the stolen gems were never found. The crime is a great mystery to the present day. The Queen remains the Sovereign of the Order, and so the jewels still belong to the crown. They were estimated to be worth about £50,000 in 1907, but their symbolic value is much greater. Their estimated value today is well over two million pounds!

"And so, young readers—this treasure hunt is a worthy candidate for you to pursue."

Carol put down the book and lent back in her chair. All was quiet, except for a few birds outside.

They remained silent for some time until Beryl simply said, "Carol. We are worth two million pounds!!!"

That was enough to set off the celebrations. The two girls ran outside, dancing and skipping, clapping and slapping, hi-fiving and cartwheeling, rolling on the grass and singing: 'We are millionaires, we are millionaires!' to the tune of 'We are family.' This went on for some time. Then they ran over to Tim's log and kissed his sign again and again, saying 'Thank you, Tim, thank you, Tim, you saved us!'

There were so many questions and so much to discuss that the girls didn't know where to start.

"We're filthy rich!" Beryl exclaimed, and followed that with, "In theory only. They belong to the Queen. But, just for now… we're the richest girls in England!"

"Just for now," Carol laughed. They high fived again, and for good measure did their special edition two-minute secret handshake.

"No wonder the thief fled Ireland and hid the Jewels," said Beryl, "who would buy them? They would be way too hot to sell. He would have had the whole of Ireland and England's police on his trail. I guess he could have sold the diamonds one by one, but it's probably worth much more as a jewel."

"Of course," Carol smacked her thigh, then winced from the pain, because it was near where Fred's stick had hit her. "Now I get it. Tim read the treasure book. When he came to the chapter about the Irish Crown Jewels, Francis Shackleton is mentioned, his hero Earnest Shackleton's younger brother. That's why he became fascinated with the Irish Crown Jewels and began investigating them. Tim was wondering what the thief would do with the jewels. Ireland is a small place, and all the people involved know or suspect one another, including the person who stole it. He had to escape. He can't go by ferry. So Tim guessed he used one of the smuggler's sea routes to escape to England. He knew about the smuggler's cave from exploring the area, so he thought it might be possible that the thief hid it in that area."

"And where is the second piece, the Badge?" Beryl asked. "They split them up. Maybe finding the Star could lead to finding the Badge."

"Let's find it!" Carol agreed.

"We better not touch the Star, there may be fingerprints on it." Beryl was in full detective mode as well.

"You're right." Carol was impressed.

"I still can't believe this at all." The girls were so excited. "Good on us. We found the jewels when no one else did—90 years on! We've cracked one of the greatest crime mysteries of all time!"

"Or at least found the loot," Carol laughed. "We'll leave the cracking for later."

"Agreed," said Beryl. "But one main question remains."

"I know. What the hell do we do now?" Carol had imagined many possible scenarios, but nothing like this.

"No doubt about it," said Beryl. "We'll give it back to the Queen."

"Most definitely," Carol agreed, "but how?"

"We'll never get through to the Queen. We have to go as high up as possible. But they probably won't believe us," Beryl said and then after some thought added, "we need a photograph."

"Let's take some now." Carol got her camera from her rucksack. "And let's hope Mr. Mundy doesn't ask any questions."

They went outside, opened the box, and extracted the jewel from the leather bag. Beryl unwrapped it, careful not to touch the back, and put it on the porch table. It shone and glittered in the evening sun, its green emeralds and red rubies accentuating the gleaming diamonds.

"It is absolutely stunning!' said Carol. She took a picture.

Then she set the timer, carefully placed the camera on the windowsill, and took a picture of both of them holding the gem— the richest girls in England.

CHAPTER 49

C arol and Beryl were bubbling over. They hid the treasure box and skipped, chattered and hi-fived all the way to their park bench office.

"We did it, we found it, we cracked it!" Carol sang.

"We are worth two million, we are worth two million!" Beryl sang and danced.

They sat on their office bench. After a while reality started sinking in.

"You know, the good thing is that it's such a stonking treasure," Beryl groaned, "but the bad thing is, it's not ours. We'll give it back, and if we're lucky we'll get a thank you letter from Her Majesty. It's probably small change for her. And that will be the end of that. So really, we are as poor as we ever were. House-wise, we haven't solved anything."

Carol knew it, and she was upset. She looked for a way out.

"We could sell it to someone else. My aunt's new husband deals with jewellery. My mum says he's a bit crooked if you know what I mean. I know he would do it for us. It's probably too hot to sell as it is, but he could break it into diamonds and emeralds and get loads of money, enough to save my house and buy a few more. We can help Mrs. E buy her house back and live in an ice-cream shop. Why not?"

They thought about it for some time. It sounded extremely tempting, and there was no logical reason why not. The Queen would never even know. Beryl imagined a house in America with a private basketball court and personal trainer, and Carol was thinking about a home in Italy with a swimming pool and library.

The girls looked at each other and knew they had reached the same conclusion.

Carol stood up.

"Let's go. We have to let the royal family know. I don't fancy keeping the jewel for too long. It could get stolen or damaged."

They took the photos to Mr. Mundy's shop and asked for express delivery.

"Can we have them digitally on a CD?"

"No problem," said Mr. Mundy. "Come back this evening before I close. That will be £4.50, please, girls."

Carol groaned. Money again. Here they were with over two million pounds in jewellery, and they didn't have five pounds to develop photos.

"Can we have it on credit, Mr. Mundy, please?" Beryl said sweetly, tossing her hair back. "We'll pay back next week, I promise."

Mr. Mundy thought for a moment and smiled.

"Don't see why not, girls," he said, "after all, I know where you live."

They crossed the street to the internet café. It wasn't really an internet café, more a café whose owner thought it would be a good idea to stick three old computers in the back. Carol got out her last 50 pence, which bought them an hour on the net. Beryl's father had warned her that computers could be traced, so they would have to work from the internet café or the library. You never knew who was watching.

They chose the furthest corner where no one could see them and sat down at the computer. First, the girls searched for the Irish Crown Jewels. They found various articles that had appeared in newspapers over the years. Most of the pictures were similar to the one in the book, though some were a little better and confirmed that they had the real Grand Master Star. Other than that, there was nothing much extra than the story in the book, although some articles went into more details about the suspects.

"We'll have to study those," said Beryl, "it might help us find out who our thief was and, more importantly, where the other jewel is, the Badge."

"Agreed," said Carol, "but one thing at a time. We only have forty-five minutes of internet left."

So they searched for 'royal family contact.'

It appeared that writing a letter to Her Majesty was quite simple. The website announced:

Writing to The Queen

You can write to Her Majesty at the following address:

Her Majesty the Queen
Buckingham Palace
London SW1A 1AA

The Queen is shown almost all of her correspondence daily by one of her Private Secretaries, and she takes a keen interest in the letters she receives.

For email correspondence, please write to:

Buckingham Palace,
Mr. Maximillian Taffler,
press officer at:
max.taffler@royal.gov.uk

"Wow, impressive!" Beryl laughed. "I bet people write: Your Majesty. My cat is stuck in a tree. Can you help?"

They spent a few minutes studying the guidelines for writing to

the royal family, then Beryl created a new email address:
johnsmith97@hotmail.com.

She typed for a few minutes, then proudly showed her letter to Carol.

Subject: Return of stolen goods.

Dear Madam,

We are two schoolgirls, even though our email says John Smith, but we are not really John Smith. Ha-ha. But we can't say our real names right now.

Through much effort and good luck, we have retrieved the royal family's Grand Master Star that was stolen in Ireland on the 6th of June 1907. We are sure you know all about it. We are great admirers of Your Royal Highness so it would be your obedient servants' honour to return it to you, the rightful owner. We are very sorry, but we have not found the Badge that goes with it (yet).

You probably think this is a hoax. Well, it isn't. We can send a picture of the Star for proof. We are sure you understand that we have to be very careful.

We look forward to your early response. (Please note that school starts in two weeks!)

Please attach proof of identity to your reply. Just so we know you are not trying to trick us.

We have the honour to be, Madam, Your Majesty's humble and obedient servants,

John Smith

Carol thought it was kind of okay, but not up to royal standards.

"I don't think we should say we are two girls. Too risky, people could ask around and find out who we are. How about two young people?"

Beryl could see her point, so that changed.

But Carol wasn't done.

"I think you should delete the *Ha-ha* bit. I'm not too sure that it's good manners when it comes to the Queen," she said. Beryl objected because she liked the *Ha-ha*, and she thought Her Majesty would like it too, but after some discussion, she reluctantly took it out.

Finally, both girls were satisfied. But they had spent 20 minutes debating and editing, so their time was almost up.

Beryl pressed 'Send' two seconds before the screen went blue, announcing that their session had ended.

"Oh, no!" said Carol, alarmed. "Did it go?"

"I don't know," Beryl replied, herself anxious. "We'll just have to wait and find out."

CHAPTER 50

As usual, Mr. Mundy had peeked at the pictures.

"Nice trinket, girls," he said. "Did you make that yourselves?"

"Made in China, Mr. Mundy," Beryl said, trying not to laugh.

"Yes, it looks cheap," said Mr. Mundy, handing them the CD.

"We'll be sure to pay you very soon," Carol promised.

"No problem, ladies," said Mr. Mundy.

"He needs a course in jewel evaluation," Carol chuckled as they left the shop.

* * *

The next morning, the two girls went to the library. That was the only place in town where they could check the internet for free.

They said hello to Mrs. Norman at the front desk and went to sit by the computer. Beryl signed in and opened the email account. There was one email.

She looked at Carol excitedly and said, "We have mail!"

Beryl opened the mail. It read:

Welcome to Hotmail! We hope you enjoy our service.
Thanks
Your friends at Hotmail

"Argh!" Beryl smacked her forehead

"Argh!" echoed Carol.

There was nothing to do but wait. The girls had no money for ice-cream, so they went to play frisbee and mess around in the park. Anything better than going home. After a few hours, they returned to the library and logged on again.

The top line announced, *'You have new mail.'*

This was it.

Beryl and Carol looked at each other excitedly, then Beryl clicked the message. The ancient computer groaned and the slow internet ground away. It was another half a minute before they got to the mail, in which time Carol's lip was nearly bleeding, and Beryl was tapping a hole in the floor with her feet. When they were finally in, Beryl looked around to make sure no one was listening and read in a whisper.

"Sender: Francis.Humphry@gov.uk
"Subject: Return of stolen goods

"Dear Mr. John Smith,

"How are both of you? Thank you very much for writing.

"I must be honest—we have received many claims of people finding the 'Irish Crown Jewels' over the years and, as you may guess, none of them has turned out to be real. Therefore, I must ask you to discontinue any further correspondence on this subject if your claim is untrue. You are, of course, aware that false claims are a criminal offence, with a penalty of six months imprisonment and a fine of five thousand pounds. We do refer all such false claims to the police who take this offence very seriously."

The girls looked at each other with alarm. That was a hefty fine, and prison didn't sound like fun. For a moment, they wondered if the Star was real.

Beryl continued reading.

"Nevertheless, we do pursue all leads and will look into your claim.

"Please send a picture of the Grand Master Star, and if it seems to be authentic, we will be delighted to meet you. I have informed Her Majesty, the Queen, of your claim, and she sends her regards. Of course, Her Majesty would be overjoyed if the jewels were found, as the Grand Master Star holds much significance to the royal family. Once again, I must emphasise that we have received many false reports.

"I attach a letter with my credentials as requested, and a picture of myself side by side with Her Royal Highness. If your assertion is true, I look forward to receiving a photograph of the Grand Master Star.

"I wish you a pleasant end of the holiday and a successful start to the school year.

Yours faithfully,

Sir Francis L. Humphry

Personal Aide to Her Majesty the Queen.

"They must think we are total nutters and cheats," she added.

"Yep, time-wasting kids," Carol agreed. "But I think you're in for a surprise, Mr. Sir Humphry."

Beryl clicked the attachment. A document opened. On top was a red logo showing a royal coat of arms. Underneath it were the words 'Buckingham Palace.'

BUCKINGHAM PALACE

Dear John Smith,   *August 12, 1997*

I have been commanded by Her Majesty the Queen to confirm that Sir Francis L. Humphry, MBE, is a trustworthy Personal Aide to Queen Elizabeth the Second.

Yours Sincerely,

Mrs. Margaret Lucy Tyler

Deputy to Senior Correspondence Officer.

The girls looked at each other. This was the real deal!

Beryl clicked on the second attachment. A photograph opened with a picture of Queen Elizabeth surrounded by several men, all dressed in smart suits. Underneath were their names and titles. Standing on the far right was a pleasant-looking tall man, his white hair neatly combed backwards. He was wearing a suit with a blue tie, and a blue handkerchief was sticking out of his breast pocket. The caption on the bottom indicated that this was indeed Sir Humphry!

"For real, for real!" Carol clapped her hands. Two people turned to look at her, so she quickly quieted down.

"Yep," said Beryl. "He could fake the letter, but not the picture, and after all, the email address we wrote to was for the royal press officer. Let's send the photo."

Carol agreed. It looked safe, but she was still thinking of any way that Sir Humphry's email could be fake. She couldn't find any, so she got the CD out of her bag and placed it in the ancient computer. The folder appeared, and Beryl clicked it open to find the pictures they had developed. She glanced around to make sure no one was looking and clicked on the first one. It was the picture of the girls holding the Jewel.

"We can't use that," she said.

"For sure not," Carol replied. "Even if we take our faces out, there may be clues in the background. They'll have the secret service knocking on our doors in no time."

The second picture was the one of the Grand Master Star on its own. It was vivid and looked very real. It was probably the best picture ever taken of the star, seeing as cameras in 1907 were not of very high quality. There was nothing other than the porch table in the background.

"This will do nicely," Beryl said. "Mr. Sir Francis Humphry, you are in for a surprise!"

She opened a reply email and wrote:

Dear Sir Humphry,

Thank you for taking the time to answer. We certainly understand that our claim would be hard to believe. Please have a look at the attached picture and see what you think. If you still don't believe us, we shall have to consider doing something else with the jewel. Perhaps selling it to a Saudi prince or wearing it at our weddings.

Yours Sincerely,

Mr. John Smith

"You can't say that!" said Carol, alarmed. "It sounds like a threat, and he would know we were girls. Anyway, we're not sure we want to get married."

They decided to leave the Saudi prince bit in but remove the wedding part. After a moment's thought, Beryl added:

We look forward to your speedy reply.

Then she attached the picture. She looked at Carol for confirmation, and Carol nodded. Beryl pressed 'Send.'

CHAPTER 51

They had nothing to do, so they surfed for a while, checking out the latest movies and basketball scores.

Ping!

The computer flashed a message:

You have new mail.

"That was quick!" said Beryl. Her hand trembled when she clicked on the message. It read:

Sender: Francis.Humphry@gov.uk
Subject: Return of stolen goods

Dear Mr. John Smith,

I hope this finds you both well.

This is quite incredible! The Grand Master Jewel looks real, and I must admit to being very surprised indeed. Unless you have managed to create an exact replica, which, however, would not be easy, as there are no quality photos of the original.

I would like to meet you as soon as possible. Please send instructions.

I will, of course, inform Her Royal Highness of these developments.

Please do be careful! If anyone finds out about this, it could attract a lot of dangerous attention.

Looking forward to your speedy reply,

Yours sincerely,

Sir Francis Humphry

Personal Aide to Her Majesty the Queen.

"Yessss," both girls hissed at the same time, followed by a short version of the secret handshake. They had caught the big fish!

"Let me drive," said Carol, nudging her friend away. "I've got this sorted."

Beryl recognised Carol's particular tone of voice. It meant that her brain had been churning fast enough to make the computer's brain dizzy. When Carol was like this, you just handed her the reins and got out of the way, so she could get on with it. She got up and moved over. Carol sat in the driver's seat and started typing furiously. It was clear that she already knew everything she was going to say. When she was finished, she showed it to Beryl, who read it carefully, then smiled. Yes! Carol did know what she was doing. She gave her the thumbs up, and Carol pressed 'Send.'

When they arrived home, just before parting Carol reminded her, "We must leave at 10:00 AM sharp. Don't be late, and don't forget the equipment. We have to be very careful; you don't mess about with a two-million-pound gem."

"Aye-aye, Captain," Beryl saluted. "See you at 10:00!"

But when Carol got home, she got hit with a sledgehammer.

"Carol," Mum said. "We are going flat hunting in Birmingham tomorrow, and we will be looking at schools for you. The buyers just told me they want to close the deal immediately, but I told them they would have to wait till right after Christmas. January the 2nd we move out. We leave tomorrow at 10:00 AM sharp, so get ready, and don't be late."

Carol tried everything, but no amount of pleading, begging, or crying helped.

CHAPTER 52

By 9:45 in the morning, Beryl was ready to go. She had a small rucksack packed with her dad's binoculars and the walkie-talkie set she got for her ninth birthday, as well as some sandwiches and water. She cleaned up her breakfast plate and walked to the door.

"Just one moment, young lady!" She heard a shrill voice that spelt trouble. Mum on the attack.

"Aren't we forgetting something?" said Mum. "We marked today as being clothes sorting day before the new school year!"

"But Mum..." Beryl stuttered, alarmed that she had forgotten all about it.

"But, but, but!" said Mum in her finest cynical voice. "No ifs or buts, young lady. I missed yoga to do this with you!"

Beryl groaned. Mum missing yoga was an unforgivable offence. Her brain spun like a hamster on a motorised treadwheel, desperately searching for a way out.

"P- P- P please, Mum," she begged. "I have basketball training. I totally forgot about the clothes. I'm so sorry. I promise you I'll do it all myself tonight. You don't have to help at all."

"Not going to happen!" said Mum with a tone that spelt finality. "Let's do this."

When Beryl's mum put her foot down, a bulldozer wouldn't budge her. Beryl was trapped—there was no way out. Except for one, and it was not a very pleasant option. Silently, she headed for the back door, well aware that this would result in a week's grounding. But Carol was counting on her, and this was their only chance to meet Mr. Sir Humphry. Sometimes you just had to do what you had to do and deal with the consequences later.

She closed the back door with her perfected silent technique and ran in a low crouch to the garden fence, which she skillfully jumped over to avoid the squeaky gate. Then she circled the house, keeping low to avoid being seen from the window. Just as she got to the road, she heard the dreaded scream she had been expecting:

"Beeeryyyyl!" Followed by a juicy and unrepeatable Finnish swear word.

Beryl ran.

It was one thing dealing with Hank or Fred, but Beryl's mum in Viking mode was a whole different category. Beryl saw Carol crouching beneath her front gate, obviously hiding as well, which was strange.

She had no time to ask why, so she just kept going at turbocharge speed, shouting, "Run Peril, run!" with Carol following closely at her heels.

They reached the park in record time, huffing and puffing.

Carol, bent over with her hands on her knees and struggling for breath, managed to ask, "Trouble at base camp? I just escaped flat hunting day in Birmingham."

Beryl, who was gasping and holding her stomach, replied, "Clothes-Day," and Carol groaned. Clothes-Day was nearly as bad as Schoolbook-Day, with a certified 9 out of 10 on the misery scale.

"Running late," Carol said. "Got to move fast. Mr. Sir Humphry will be here at 12 noon, but we have to be ready well before that, in case it's someone else and they come early to ambush us. Now, remember the three signs, and stand by to get a signal from me on each."

Beryl handed Carol the binoculars and one walkie-talkie. They did a soundcheck, which worked well, and then Beryl, still gasping for air, ran towards the far corner of the park and the forest edge. She was so winded and rushed that she forgot to look around to make sure no one was watching. As it later turned out, somebody was watching.

Three somebodies.

Carol got a hoodie out of her rucksack and put it on, then settled down to wait.

At precisely 11:59 AM, she saw the Bentley driving slowly down the road, coming from the opposite end of the park. It stopped behind a large bush where people would not notice it, just as Carol had instructed in her email. She got out her binoculars and looked. It was a special edition Bentley, painted in deep claret maroon. She checked the registration plate. There was none, the Queen's cars needed no registration. Perfect. Any other vehicle without a licence plate would be stopped by the police on its way from London. Then she looked at the front of the car. There it was—a silver mascot of St. George slaying the dragon. No doubt about it, this was one of the royal fleet cars. Two men were sitting in front. In the passenger seat, she could see Sir Humphry with his white hair combed back, just as in the picture. Behind the steering wheel was a man wearing a dark suit and tie and a chauffeur's cap with the royal staff badge pinned in front.

She made sure there was no one around, then she got the walkie-talkie out of her pocket and pressed the beep button once. A moment later, she got a return beep from Beryl acknowledging that Mr. Sir Humphry had passed the first test.

Carol put the binoculars away and pulled her hood up. She got the envelope she had prepared out of her inner pocket. Then Carol casually walked towards the car, using her special edition lazy-school-girl lope. As she passed the car, she quickly reached out and stuck the envelope under the windscreen wiper blade, picked up speed, and before the men realised it, she was gone. Carol headed around the back path to their bench, where she took out the walkie-talkie and beeped twice, letting Beryl know the message had been delivered. A moment later, she got three return beeps, signalling that Beryl had been to the Meukki and was on her way back with the Star. Carol pulled the hoodie over her head and settled down to wait.

After two minutes, she saw Mr. Sir Humphry walking down the path, studying the map she had drawn for him. Carol looked around to make sure he was alone. She had a good view of the park and could easily see that no one was following him. She sat calmly but was ready to run the instant something went wrong.

Mr. Sir Humphry walked over to the bench and stood by Carol. He smelled of delicate but expensive aftershave. She was looking at the ground with her head covered so he could not see her face.

She stuck out her hand and mumbled "Letter" in a deep, muffled voice.

Mr. Sir Humphry pulled an envelope out of his inner pocket and handed it to Carol. It was sealed with a red wax seal. She took it from him, tore it open, and pulled the letter out. It was typed on expensive paper. She read without looking up:

BUCKINGHAM PALACE

To Mr. John Smith,

I hereby certify that the man standing in front of you is Sir Francis Humphry, my Personal Aide.

Sincerely,

Elizabeth Alexandra Mary

Her Majesty Queen of England.

Carol examined the signature. It was definitely the Queen's; she had studied it carefully on the internet. On top of it was the royal stamp in red wax.

One last test.

"Passport," Carol mumbled in her muffled voice. Mr. Sir Humphry handed her the document. It was a special edition royal passport. She opened it to the first page, and there it was: the name Sir Francis Humphry and above it a picture of the man standing before her. He had passed the final test; there was no doubt he was the real thing.

Carol stood up, took off her hoodie, curtsied, stuck her hand out, smiled a huge grin, and declared in her best posh accent, "Sir

Francis Humphry, I presume?"

Sir Humphry smiled at Carol kindly. She liked him immediately.

He shook her hand firmly and said in a genuine posh accent, "Indeed. Mr. John Smith, I presume?"

Carol gestured at the bench and said, "Welcome to my office, Sir Humphry. Please do have a seat. My real name is Carol."

"Very pleased to meet you, Carol," said Sir Humphry, sitting on the bench. "Please call me Francis. What a lovely office you have."

Carol sat down beside him, and Sir Humphry asked, "So my dear, two weeks of holiday left. How was your summer?"

Carol liked the fact that he didn't ask her about the jewel immediately. It would have been poor manners.

"To be honest, sir, this has been the most wonderful, difficult, and exciting adventure I could ever imagine having on a summer holiday. But having you here means it has all ended well, which is truly a miracle."

Sir Humphry appeared very interested.

"I would love to hear all about it," he said.

"It was a treasure hunt with many challenges, but we passed them all."

"Then it must be due to your courage, perseverance, and cleverness. But tell me please, where is the other Mr. John Smith?"

Carol had almost forgotten about Beryl.

"She's waiting nearby with the Grand Master Star, sir," she said. "Would you like to see it?"

"Indeed, I would," said Sir Humphry.

Carol pressed five long beeps on the walkie-talkie.

Beryl had just arrived at the edge of the forest. In her rucksack was the leather pouch with the Star. Beryl was grateful she had removed it from the heavy tin box, she was winded and panting as it was. Having escaped her mum, raced to the park, and ran to the Meukki and back, she felt as though she had run a marathon. Her lungs were burning, and her legs were cramped and aching.

When she heard the five beeps, she breathed a sigh of relief. Finally, it would all be over. She stood up stiffly, still catching her breath, and responded with five long beeps. Then she picked up the rucksack and walked out of the forest.

And there, standing right in front of her with nasty grins on their faces, were the High-Street Gang.

CHAPTER 53

Beryl froze, paralysed with fear. Her first thought was the rucksack with the treasure inside. If the Gang took it off her, it would all be over. Their whole treasure hunt would be in vain, and worse still, the boys would get all the money and the credit. Her situation was not looking good. In fact, it was looking horrible. The boys were blocking her way, she was alone, and they were looking meaner than ever.

"Well, well, well," said fat Ernest with a sneer. "Look what we have here! If it isn't our friend Beryl without her buddy Peril to look after her. Caught you on your own, have we?"

Simon snickered, "Yes, it's lesson time. What's the matter, Beryl? Not sticking your tongue out? Maybe you lost it? Don't worry. When we've finished with you, you'll be tasting the ground with it."

Judging by their laughter, it appeared the boys considered this remark amazingly witty.

Gimpy felt he had to add his two pence worth of bully humour and said,

"And when we finish with you, we'll give your friend Peril a taste of our fists, too!"

The boys roared with laughter.

That was their mistake. Like all bullies, they tended to talk too much. By this time, Beryl had gotten over her initial shock and managed to get her breathing under control. No point in running back to the forest, they would catch her before she could hide.

Beryl had learnt one important lesson from basketball and backgammon. If you were cornered with no way out, attack was the best defence. So she pictured herself on a basketball court, with the three bullies as the opposing team's defensive line and the basket just behind them. She imagined she had to get through to the basket, and that meant a 'cut' play. She chose the Backdoor-Cut. She picked the slowest and stupidest of the three, which was Earnie, standing to her left.

Casually, she tossed the walkie-talkie at him and shouted, "Catch!"

Earnie fell for it. He held both hands out to catch the walkie-talkie, missed, and looked down while it fell to the ground. The three boys had their eye on the walkie-talkie, rather than on Beryl, and she seized the moment. She ran straight at Earnie with her left arm outstretched, pushing him to the left, and then rapidly and unexpectedly swerved to the right, running between Gimpy and Simon. The boys were taken by surprise. They had expected Beryl to run away from them, not at them.

Beryl ran towards the park, which was a few hundred metres away and hidden behind a clump of trees, but she was slowing down. The bullies gave chase, shouting threats and abuse, and were gaining on her. Beryl realised she could not outrun the boys anymore. She turned to face them, pretended to throw the rucksack to the right, then suddenly veered left in an L-cut, passing them again. The boys were no match for Beryl's basketball skills and fitness, and after a few minutes they were bending over, hands on knees, huffing and puffing. But it was three against one, and Beryl was exhausted. She had never run so far in her life, and she would not be able to keep it up much longer.

If she could just get to the bench, maybe Sir Humphry would help. No, he was probably way too old and posh to deal with three rough bullies. He would leave, and the meeting would be ruined. It would be Carol and her against the three boys, and Beryl was worn out. They would take the treasure from them, and everything would be lost. She heard a shout from behind and looked back with alarm. The boys had recovered and were running towards her at full speed and getting dangerously close. She had to get to the bench.

Beryl turned to run, but her legs cramped and seized up. Her heart was pounding, her lungs were on fire, and she had no air left. She opened her mouth to scream just as a hand grabbed her shirt, and she felt a strong punch on the back. She fell, and a second later fists were battering her all over. One of the boys grabbed the rucksack and tried to take it off her. If he got it, everything the girls had worked so long and so hard for would be lost. She held onto it for dear life, but he kept pulling, the straps cutting deep into her shoulders. It would not be long before he had it.

* * *

Back at the bench office, Carol and Sir Humphry sat waiting for Beryl and the treasure. Carol was surprised that Beryl had not yet arrived and was getting worried. She should have been there by now, what could be the cause of her delay?

"I don't know what has happened to my friend," Carol said with some concern in her voice.

Sir Humphry nodded with understanding, but Carol could tell he was getting sceptical. No Beryl and no Star. He was probably thinking this was a tall story after all.

He was.

"At this point, miss, I have to remind you that wasting royal staff time is a serious criminal offence. If this is not real, I will have to call the police," he said sternly.

For a brief moment, Carol thought of running away, she could easily outpace the old man. But Beryl wasn't safe. She had to stay.

"Sorry, sir, I'm getting very worried, my friend should have arrived by now." She could see Sir Humphry doubting that there ever was a friend, but at the moment she was more concerned about Beryl. She picked up the walkie-talkie and beeped five times. Perhaps Beryl had not heard her, though Carol was sure she had replied with five beeps earlier. She waited a moment when suddenly a voice came over her walkie-talkie. There was no mistake about this—it was Simon's voice.

"That you, Peril?" The voice came in from the receiver. He sounded breathless, as though he had been running. "We have your friend, and as soon as we finish beating her up, we're coming for you. In the park, are you? See you in a minute for a good whacking!"

Carol could hear Beryl screaming and crying in pain, both from the walkie-talkie and a couple of hundred metres away, behind the trees. She stood up in shock. This had all gone horribly wrong.

She looked at Sir Humphry with an expression of dismay on her face.

"The bullies have her!" She exclaimed. Carol expected Sir Humphry to get up and leave as quickly as he could. He was not a young man, and she would be astonished if he wanted to get involved with local riff-raff—not suitable for the royal name.

But instead, Sir Humphry did something very surprising.

He stood up, put two fingers in his mouth, and gave an unexpectedly loud whistle. In less than a second, Carol saw the chauffeur shooting out from behind the bushes on her left and running towards them. He was tall, well-built, and extremely agile. Sir Humphry pointed in the direction of the trees. The Chauffeur didn't even stop. Five seconds later he was halfway there, running at an unbelievable speed and looking like a leopard on the hunt. Two seconds more and he had vanished behind the trees.

Carol ran after him. As she drew near, she saw Gimpy flying

into the air and landing on his back. Simon was holding his ear and crying. By the time she got there, the Chauffeur was holding Earnie up by the collar, shaking him as if he were a rag doll and saying in a tough London accent,

"Listen carefully, mate. If I ever catch you bothering these young women again, you will be very, very sorry for a long, long time. I work for her Majesty's special guard, and I will know how to find you. Am I making myself perfectly clear?" He yanked Earnie further in the air.

"No, sir, sorry, sir, I mean yes, sir… we promise never to bother them again," Earnie groaned, wiggling his legs hopelessly as he tried to feel the ground beneath him.

"Ever?" The Chauffeur gave him a shake.

"Ever," Earnie mumbled, now in tears.

The Chauffeur let go, and Earnie fell to the ground, but not before he got a powerful blow to the ear. He yelped in pain.

"Then get out of here now, and don't let me see you again, or else!" the Chauffeur said in a low growling tone.

Three frightened bullies turned and ran. And they didn't stop running for a long, long time.

CHAPTER 54

The four of them stood around the 'office' bench. Beryl was trembling and breathing heavily, both from the running and from fright. Carol's heart was galloping, and she was thanking heaven that Beryl and the treasure were safe. Sir Humphry and the Chauffeur were waiting patiently with concerned looks on their faces.

After a few minutes, the girls regained their composure and were able to talk again.

"Please allow me to introduce the second Mr. John Smith," Carol said. "John, this is Sir Francis Humphry."

Beryl curtsied, shook Sir Humphry's hand, and said, "Very pleased to meet you, sir. You may call me Beryl."

"Very pleased to meet you, Beryl," Sir Humphry smiled.

Beryl liked Sir Humphry. He seemed kind and friendly, and he treated the girls like adults rather than kids.

"This is my chauffeur, Robert," Sir Humphry introduced the tall man. "He is also a trained commando and my bodyguard." Of course, Carol thought. Mr. Sir Humphry would not come unprotected.

Robert nodded.

"Pleasure to meet you, Carol, Beryl," he said, shaking the girls' hands. His hand was massive. "Well done for your slick operation back there, very professional. Just make sure your binoculars don't reflect the sun next time."

Carol blushed from pride and embarrassment.

Beryl looked at Robert and said, "Thank you for saving me. I couldn't have lasted a second longer, they were running after me for ages and nearly got the rucksack."

"Well done for lasting that long." Sir Humphry said with a tone of admiration "How did you manage, one against three?"

Beryl smiled. "All I can say, sir, is thank goodness for basketball cut play."

Sir Humphry and Carol looked puzzled by this, but Robert grinned and said, "Backdoor-Cut, V-Cut, L-Cut, sir, standard basketball evasion tactics." He knew his stuff.

Sir Humphry nodded.

"I'm sure you are very eager to see the Grand Master Star, sir," said Beryl, sitting cross-legged on the grass in front of the bench and placing the rucksack on her lap.

"Indeed, I am more than intrigued," admitted Sir Humphry.

"Do you think this is the real thing, sir, or do you think we're a hoax?" she asked out of curiosity.

"Well, to be honest, I had serious doubts until a few moments ago. But now that I have met you, I believe it may just be possible. It will be truly incredible if you have found the Star."

Beryl said nothing. Instead, she pulled the leather pouch out of the rucksack and placed it on the ground between them. Robert looked around to make sure no one was there. The park was empty.

"You have to be careful while touching it, sir. There may be fingerprints."

Sir Humphry nodded. "Good thinking, best to be careful."

Beryl took the leather pouch out of her rucksack, pulled open the drawstring and extracted an object wrapped in wax paper. She handed it to Mr. Sir Humphry. He carefully unwrapped it.

And there it was—the Grand Master Star of the Order of

Saint Patrick.

Sir Humphry stared at the impressive piece of jewellery. His jaw dropped, and his eyes opened wide in surprise. He tried to say something, but nothing came out. He closed his eyes and opened them again as if to make sure he was awake. The girls sat perfectly still, anxious not to disturb Sir Humphry and eager to hear his verdict.

Finally, Sir Humphry picked the jewel up, holding it by the edges. He stared at it for a long time and said, "This is truly astonishing. After 90 years, you have found the Grand Master Star! I don't know how you managed to pull this off, but it could not have been easy. I must congratulate you both. I can assure you that the Queen will be delighted. After all, King Edward the VII and Queen Alexandra, who reigned at the time the Star was stolen, were her great-grandfather and great-grandmother. She was always anxious to retrieve the jewels, but with so many years gone by, she had lost hope. You are going to make one Queen immensely happy today!"

Beryl and Carol were bursting with pride.

Sir Humphry examined the Star. "Isn't it a gorgeous piece of craftsmanship?" he said. "Nearly 400 Brazilian diamonds and in the middle the emerald shamrock and the ruby cross. Magnificent. The original stones were taken from the Crown Jewels of Queen Charlotte. I am sure you know by now that '*Quis Separabit?*' means 'Who will separate us?' This is a beautiful piece of royal history. The value of the stones today is well over two million pounds, but of course, the real value of the Star is much, much higher. I have to commend you both for being honest enough to return it to its rightful owners. You could have been quite rich!"

"To be perfectly honest, sir, we were dreaming of buying our own ice cream shop," Beryl said seriously.

Sir Humphry chuckled.

"With your talents, I am sure you will have more than enough ice cream in your lives. Now, I would love to hear your story. Still, it is extremely dangerous to be outside with such a valuable piece of jewellery. You were right to be cautious. Therefore, before I go, I have one request. I would like you to refrain from talking about this to anyone. The Badge is still missing, and the police will be eager to launch an investigation. We will keep this to ourselves. Therefore, there is a need for the utmost secrecy. I am sure you understand."

"We certainly understand, sir," Beryl replied in her best upper-class English. "But may I ask if this includes our parents? So far, we have not told them a thing."

"*Especially* your parents." Sir Humphry smiled. "Parents are very proud of their children and can hardly stop themselves from boasting. When the time comes, I will help you to explain."

"Not a word shall pass our lips," Beryl promised, and Carol agreed.

Sir Humphry turned to Robert and said, "Time to bring this magnificent jewel safely home to Her Majesty, where it belongs. We have to be careful, it's worth a fortune."

"Yes, sir." Robert scanned the park again to make sure no one was there. Then he turned to the two girls and saluted. "Beryl, Carol, you have done a very professional job. I hope to see you in the Special Forces one day."

Beryl and Carol stood straight and saluted smartly back.

"I hope you will hear from us, but it may take quite some time. Issues such as this move very slowly in Buckingham Palace." Sir Humphry told them before leaving. "We have to check the jewel to properly verify it, and the detectives will want to investigate and search for the Badge. Meanwhile, remember, not a word to anyone." He nodded to Robert, who took the rucksack with the box, looked around carefully, and before they knew it, the two men were gone.

Beryl and Carol looked at each other and sighed.

"Well, I dare say!" said Beryl, still in her posh accent.

Carol laughed. "You can stop talking Mr. Sir Humphry now."

"Very well, my dear," Beryl continued in her best English. "I suppose that *is* that."

Finally, their mission was complete. The treasure was safe and had been delivered to its rightful owner. The girls felt strange and, for a moment, a bit empty. They looked at each other, sighed, smiled, hugged, and did the extra-long version of their secret handshake. It was a special moment.

"That is that," said Carol. "Well done for us, and now back to real life."

"Oh my God!!" Beryl jumped up. "Real life. My mum! Run."

They ran.

When they were nearly at the gate, Beryl said, "Best summer of our lives. You probably won't see me for a week, but I hope I'm out of prison in time to enjoy the end of the holidays in the Meukki with you."

Carol hugged her and said, "See you there, sister mine. May the force be with you when fighting the evil powers of Clothes-Day. Good luck." She stood by the gate and watched her friend walk down the garden path and through the front door, where she was swallowed by the dark side.

CHAPTER 55

The days were growing shorter and the shadows longer. Autumn was in the air. Brown leaves were scattered around the clearing, and the occasional wind or drizzle threw shivers into the girls' spines. It had been a glorious English summer, but now it was migrating south with the birds.

It was the last day of the holidays. After a dreadful week of being grounded in their rooms, there were only two days of holiday left. Beryl and Carol had spent yesterday, Saturday, enjoying their little house and garden. They lounged on the grass, had a picnic, played games, and jumped from their swing into the now chilly waters of the river.

Today they had buttoned down the hatches for winter, closing windows, packing things away, and making sure nothing was left outside. They would still come and visit on weekends, but so would the rains and snows, so they had to make sure all was safe. Lastly, they pulled the Kon-Taki on to the riverbank and stowed it away.

When all was done, the two girls sat on the porch of their little house, looking at their beloved clearing and chatting about the adventures of the last few months.

"You know something strange?" Carol said. "We should thank the High-Street Gang for all of this."

"I was thinking the same thing," Beryl replied. "Like, we would never have come into the forest and found the clearing *or* built the

Meukki *or* found Tim's box and the treasure."

Carol raised her teacup. "Here's to the bully boys. Even the baddest, worst things can lead to something good."

They talked about everything except the issue that was just too painful to talk about. After Christmas, Carol would move to the city. She would be stuck in a tiny flat with her mum and Jerry. She had just been informed that her father would have to remain in Cambridge for a year or more. There was no teaching post in Birmingham, and they could not afford to move to expensive Cambridge with him.

Without her dad to cheer her up, all Carol could see ahead was gloom and doom. As for Beryl, the horrible Gimpy would move next door, and she would be left alone to deal with him and his friends. Beryl shivered at the thought.

It was now certain that the textile factory was shutting down in the new year. Shops would close, people would leave town, and Londoners would buy second homes for their two-week vacations. The girls had done all they could to save the situation, but they had failed. The only glimmer of hope was the hospice. If it were a success, Carol's mother might get a job in their accounting department; it might just save their house and the town.

Beryl and Carol had heard nothing from Mr. Sir Humphry, and they weren't surprised. He had told them it might take ages. For one glorious week, they had been millionaires, and now they were back to being two poor girls. But if they had made the Queen happy, that was the best reward. They had enjoyed the journey, and it had been the best journey ever; the treasure could enjoy itself.

They chatted and joked for a while longer, trying to stretch the last precious moments of freedom. Tomorrow, it would be back to Old Jackson's history and Scruffy Duffy's maths, English and French and exams, but also friends, sports, and play. Holidays were long and tended to blur time, so it was nice to have a break from them too.

It was late afternoon, but dusk was falling much earlier now, and it was time to go home. The girls checked the Meukki one more time. The bed was made, the table was clean, the books were stacked on the shelves and the tools packed away. They closed the door behind them, waved goodbye to Tim, and headed home.

The date was Sunday the 31st of August 1997, the day Princess Diana was killed in a car crash.

CHAPTER 56

Autumn was grinding into winter. Coats, scarves, and gloves had come out of attics, and the end of term exams were looming dangerously close. Carol pulled the duvet over her head, grabbing a few more minutes of sleep and warmth before the shock of a cold floor and bathroom. But the shrill voice of her mother calling from downstairs put a stop to her hibernation attempts. She wondered why Mum was waking her on Saturday. Not fair! Then she remembered. First house packing day—sorting out old books and clothes. Horrible.

Carol dragged herself out of bed and changed into clothes as fast as she could to prevent herself from becoming an iceberg. She wiped the steam off the window and peeped outside. Rain, fog, and more rain, just as it has been for the last six weeks. She could see the new 'For Sale' sign outside Mrs. E's house. It turned out the London buyers were just after a quick investment and not even a second home. After Christmas, it would be sold for a nice profit. Poor Mrs. E! She had heard her mother say that Mrs. E hated living in the city and desperately wanted to move back but couldn't afford it. Just like her own family. Carol missed her father so much—it has been nearly eight months since he moved to Cambridge, though he had been home for summer. She knew from the sound of his voice on the phone he missed her, too.

For a moment, and not for the first time, she wished they had sold the jewel. Then she sighed, knowing that was never going to happen.

She glanced at the calendar above her bed. It was the 8th of November. One month exactly since the hospice 'grand opening' had been cancelled, and with it all hopes for the town. Just over a month and a half to Christmas. And then what? Stuff the house into cardboard boxes and move to the city, leaving her best friend to deal with her worst enemy. The whole term had been depressing, with Princess Di's death, the hospice failure, and people losing jobs. Carol had been crying a lot.

The house was freezing, so Carol put on a warm sweater and dragged herself downstairs, hoping for a quick slice of toast before sorting books began.

Instead, she was greeted by a grand breakfast plate with scrambled eggs, rye bread, smoked salmon, and avocado. Something was up. Her mum didn't usually make that kind of breakfast, more like 'grab-your-own-cornflakes.' Beside her plate was a vase with a rose in and propped against it was an envelope.

"Sorry, sleeping beauty," Mum called from the kitchen. "I woke you up because a mysterious letter arrived for you." Carol detected a note of excitement in Mum's voice. Strange, Mum wouldn't usually get excited about a letter.

Then she saw why. On the top right-hand corner of the envelope was the royal insignia of Buckingham Palace, and her name was beautifully written in real ink from a fountain pen. On the back was a red wax seal stamped with the royal emblem, with a small red ribbon coming out of it.

"What's this all about?" Mum came out of the kitchen, drying her hands and dying of curiosity.

Carol could only begin to guess, but she put on a surprised face.

"Don't know," she shrugged. "Maybe the royal family is trying to sell mugs with the Queen Mother's picture on." She was worried because she hadn't told her parents anything about her summer adventures.

Carefully, Carol carefully tore open the seal of the envelope and took out the letter. Her mum was falling over herself trying to see its contents. The letter was written on fancy, cream colored, textured paper. On the top right corner was the red stamp of Buckingham Palace.

She read aloud.

"Dear Carol,

"Every year the Queen awards one or two young people with a special medal for services to crown and country. We are delighted to inform you that this year, your friend Beryl and you have been selected to receive this honour. You are, therefore, invited to join the Queen for afternoon tea and a ceremony. Enclosed is a formal invitation.

"You may now explain to your parents why you have received this honour. Please apologise on my behalf and assure them it was I who requested your absolute discretion on this matter. I promise to make it up to them with a splendid time in London.

"Should you accept this invitation, you and your parents are invited to stay at the Savoy Hotel, London, for the nights of the 21st and 22nd of December 1997, at the expense of Her Majesty the Queen. This will include a visit to the theatre. I will also be delighted to give your group a guided tour of Buckingham Palace.

"We very much hope your two families will accept this invitation. Her Majesty is looking forward to meeting you all.

"Finally, we ask you to keep this visit confidential, for reasons you

will surely understand and may now explain to your parents.

"Yours Sincerely,

Sir Francis Humphry

Personal Aide to HRH Queen Elizabeth.

RSVP."

Fifteen seconds later, Carol's mum was on the phone. She needn't have bothered calling. You could hear Beryl's mum's excited screams halfway down the road.

CHAPTER 57

Beryl and Carol's parents sat in the lobby, soaking up the atmosphere. They were having the time of their lives. The Savoy was by far the most luxurious hotel they had ever visited. It was an Edwardian building, adorned with art deco style. The furnishing was classic and glamorous: car-sized chandeliers, plush furniture, and beautifully tiled floors all made them feel part of a grander, more prosperous world. Smartly dressed waiters with posh accents attended their every need. The rooms were humongous and had the most comfortable beds they had ever slept in. It did not take long until they all felt very much at home.

The only fly in the ointment was that they could not tell friends and family about the forthcoming visit to Buckingham Palace and their meeting with the Queen. After all, at least half the fun, perhaps most of the fun, was casual bragging in the manner of, 'Oh, yes, we did visit Queen Liz at the Palace yesterday.' But Sir Humphry had requested they not mention a thing about the trip, and they understood and respected that. The saga of the Irish Crown Jewels would not be over until the Badge was retrieved. Since the girls had found the Grand Master Star, there were new avenues of investigations, so the story had to be kept under wraps for now. Instead, they took loads of photographs, looking forward to the day they could show them off to their friends. They would be the talk of the town!

Beryl and Carol's parents had long since forgiven the girls

for not telling them about the Grand Master Star. After all, if the Queen's right-hand man had said keeping the story secret was the proper thing for the girls to do, who were they to disagree? What their parents did not know is that the girls had told the tale on a 'need-to-know-basis,' carefully leaving out parts of the story that would make them anxious or angry. No mention of getting lost in the Forbidden Forest, of the Meukki, Tim, Hank, or Fred. From their parents' point of view, their genius daughters had worked the whole thing out and found the treasure by themselves. Tim would understand and forgive them.

Beryl and Carol's room was six times the size of their little house. Yesterday had been the most fun day of their lives. They spent half an hour jumping on the massive bed, ate all the chocolates in the minibar, and watched Christmas movies on the giant TV. Then they shopped for clothes and visited Madame Tussauds, where they met the royal family, Elvis, and the Beatles in wax form. In the evening, they ate sushi for the first time, then saw the musical *Cats*, and finished with cake and hot chocolate at the famous 'Patisserie Valerie.' London was dressed up for Christmas, decorated with green, red, and gold streetlights and pretty Christmas trees. This morning they had wandered alongside the Thames and watched street shows, jugglers, magicians, Santa Clauses, and stand-up comics. Eventually, they reached Trafalgar Square and Nelson's Column, where lots of young people, tourists, and pigeons were all having fun. After lunch, they visited the hairdresser to prepare for their appointment with the Queen that afternoon. They had to agree that, though they were not keen on cities, London was an exception—they loved it.

Now the time had finally come to visit the palace, and the two families were bubbling with excitement. They all looked super-smart and glamorous. Beryl and Carol were dazzling in their long flowing dresses and elegant hairstyles that made them look grown-up and sophisticated. Their parents were suitably dressed up for the occasion, dads in brand new suits and mums in sweeping dresses and small hats. They looked like royalty themselves and had quite a few heads turning their way.

The girls had practised curtsies until their knees hurt. They had received precise instructions about the rules and etiquette of visiting the Queen. Curtsy and shake her hand carefully, but otherwise never touch the Queen, call her Your Majesty first and later Ma'am, don't talk or eat before the Queen does, don't turn your back on Her Majesty, don't take pictures, don't ask personal questions, remain calm, stick to small talk. There were so many rules. It would be difficult not to go wrong.

At precisely 4:30 PM, two royal Bentleys drew up outside the Savoy. The other guests noticed them immediately. Sir Humphry entered the lobby looking tall and noble in his sharply tailored suit, his white hair combed neatly backwards. The lobby fell silent; everyone knew when royalty was there. He walked over to their group and introduced himself to the girls' parents with a friendly handshake and a smile. He seemed to know who everyone was and addressed them each by name.

Then he turned to the girls and gave them a warm handshake saying, "Well, hello there, Mr. John Smith." Their parents looked puzzled. "Follow me, please," he said, and the two families made their way towards the cars. Every eye in the lobby was on them, which gave their parents a tremendous amount of pleasure. Each family entered one of the Bentleys, which had huge, beige leather seats and a brand-new smell. Beryl recognised Robert in the driver's seat, and he winked at her in the mirror.

The journey to the palace was a dream. They drove up the famous 'Mall Avenue' and through the palace gates, where the cars parked in front of the main building. Outside were troopers of the Queen's guard in traditional black and red uniform, standing so still they reminded the girls of the wax museum. Sir Humphry opened the door and escorted them into the grand entrance. The two families looked around, hardly believing their eyes. It was a magnificent hall, full of colossal marble columns, the floor covered with rich red carpeting. From somewhere above, an orchestra was playing a light waltz.

They were led up the grand staircase with its ornate gold bannisters and into the Grand Gallery, a long room with the most impressive collection of beautiful paintings. Overhead hung a chandelier that dwarfed the one at the Savoy, and at the far end was an exquisitely carved fireplace decorated with beautiful Christmas floral arrangements. At the centre of the hall stood a giant Christmas tree, twinkling with a thousand lights and red and gold decorations. From here they entered the white drawing-room, with more amazing chandeliers, yellow and gold furniture, and a magnificent gold-colored grand piano. The families were spellbound. For some reason, Carol had a flashback to the first time they saw their clearing.

The staff arranged the families in a semi-circle, where they waited with growing anticipation. The ladies were making last-minute adjustments to their hats, and the men were straightening their ties. Suddenly, as if on cue, the music stopped, and the participants were signalled that this was the moment.

The room fell silent, and the Queen, who seemed to appear from nowhere, walked slowly and gracefully in. She was wearing a pale blue twin set with a matching handbag. She looked regal but relaxed, with a gentle smile. The Queen made her way slowly around the room, greeting every guest personally as they bowed and curtsied, and taking a few moments to chat with each of their parents.

The Queen seemed to know who they all were, and the girls marvelled at her friendly attitude, extensive knowledge, sharp wit, and excellent memory. She commanded great respect while somehow allowing people to feel at ease. The Queen chatted with Isaac about science and philosophy, with Carl about the publishing world, and with Naomi about which vegetables were best to plant in the coming January. Then she spoke to Maria.

"I understand you practise natural medicine. Well done," she said. "I hope you include homoeopathy. You know that the royal family has used it for generations with great success. It's the secret of our longevity, I'm sure. I even treat my Corgis with remedies."

Maria was delighted. "It works like magic," she said enthusiastically. "So strange that some people refuse to even consider using it."

The Queen smiled with the air of one who had seen it all before and remarked, "Well, my dear, its time will come. The magic of today is the science of tomorrow."

Finally, the Queen turned to the two girls, and with a kind smile said, "So, you are the two young ladies I have heard so much about. I have been looking forward to meeting you. It is my pleasure to invite you for a cup of tea and a chat, while my staff show your parents around the palace."

The Queen turned and walked towards a door in the side of the hall. Beryl and Carol followed a few steps behind, doing their best to keep all the rules.

The room was small compared to the hall, but still about as big as Beryl's house and beautifully decorated with antique furniture. They stood facing the Queen in the centre of the room.

She looked at them and said, "Carol and Beryl, the royal family and I are in great debt to both of you for what you have accomplished. The Grand Master Star is part of our heritage, and having it stolen from my great-grandfather has been a heartbreaking tragedy. I find it quite incredible that you have managed to find it, whereas the whole British constabulary has failed to do so for the last 90 years. No doubt, you have shown great courage and ingenuity. Above all, you have been loyal. These are exactly the qualities I expect from my knights. It is my pleasure to award you both with knighthoods of the Most Illustrious Order of Saint Patrick.

"For now, I am told by the police that we must keep the whole affair secret, and I do not want people questioning the reasons for your knighthood. You may tell your parents only. But rest assured, one day the whole of England and the world will learn of what you have done."

The girls were astounded but managed to stay calm on the outside. The Queen picked up a small tray from a side table. On it were two medals with red and gold ribbons. They were the same design as the Grand Master Star, with the green shamrock and a red cross in the middle. The Queen stepped forward, and the girls bowed their heads as she hung the medals over their necks.

It was the proudest moment of their lives.

They waited for the Queen to sit, then took the two seats she gestured at. The Queen rang a tiny bell, and a waiter appeared with a tray of tea, scones, and a variety of jams. They sipped and ate the scones while the Queen asked them some questions about their adventures and listened to their story with great interest.

When they had finished, the Queen said, "Beryl and Carol. You know that the Grand Master Star is worth millions of pounds, but for the royal family, it is invaluable. We realise you could have sold it yourselves, but you chose honesty and integrity, which are much more valuable than any treasure. You may not be aware that King Edward offered a substantial reward for anyone who returned the jewel."

No. The girls had not been aware of that.

The Queen continued, "I am delighted to award each one of you a prize of 75,000 pounds."

The effect was like hitting Beryl and Carol with an electrified baseball bat. They were too stunned to say thank you, so they just nodded.

The Queen sat back in her chair. "Now, is there anything else at all that I can do for you?"

Carol had been hoping for this opportunity.

She asked, "Ma'am, does the palace by any chance need any textiles? You see, we have this textile factory in our town…"

The Queen smiled and elegantly pointed at the enormous windows and long flowing curtains.

"This is a big palace. And the royal family owns several more, all with many huge windows with curtains and drapes. Consider it done. I look forward to having you visit me at Balmoral castle in Scotland for some hiking and horse riding. And now, your parents must be getting worried. I wish you and your families a Merry Christmas and a Happy Hanukkah."

The girls curtsied, walked backwards for a few steps, and returned to their parents.

Carol's mother was bursting with curiosity.

"What medal did you get?!" she asked when she saw the ribbon and star on Carol's dress.

Carol grinned and said simply, "You may call me Dame, Mother."

THE END

Ω

ACKNOWLEDGMENTS

Thank you!

To my four Gorgeous Girlies, who inspired this story out of me and carried me all the way through:
Ella Naomi, Tilly Jane, Noga Lily, and Amy Grace
and to Louis and Ike for being the world's best brothers.
To Ella for excellent proofreading, advice, agent searching, and encouragement throughout. And for crying even on the 70th read.
To Jennie for the good times and raising amazing kids together. And for taking me to Snowdonia.
To my niece, Talya Baldwin, for the beautiful illustrations and cover.
To Rebecca Stirrup for proofreading, editing, and laughing with the girls.
To my cuz, Nicole Tibbetts, for great editing and advice.
To John Fox from Bookfox for inspirational content editing.
To Mark Malatesta for helping me make this a tighter book and guiding me on the path to publication.
To Simon Hough for excellent formatting and preparing for press.
To Naomi Langford for basketball coaching.
To Anne Baker for bird advice.
To Ekaterina, who started me writing this book.

To all my friends and relatives who read the book and loved it. You all kept me going.

To my wife, Camilla, for entering the forest with me and sharing the adventure. You tiger, me owl.

And to me for allowing myself a break from writing professional homoeopathic books. I had such fun! It's great being a child.

Made in United States
Orlando, FL
07 January 2023

28346547R00150